Bex Kilburn is the pen name of an aspiring horror filmmaker, whose work has screened across a number of international genre festivals.

Off Duty started its life as a short film, which toured multiple countries in 2018-19, and was written and directed by the author.

Bex continues to make short horror films in her spare time, but has now realised the joys of creating stories without having to worry about the budget.

@bexkilburn

www.bexkilburn.com

OFF DUTY

BEX KILBURN

PULSE
BOOKS

INTRODUCTION

One of the unusual things about this book is that it didn't start out as a book at all.

In the spring of 2018, I had access to three important things - a police uniform, a warehouse in Basildon, and a crew of people mad enough to enjoy making horror films at the weekend with me.

So, from one Friday evening as the warehouse closed down for the weekend, to the early hours of Monday morning when the first delivery arrived, we shot a story about a young female police officer who could talk to ghosts.

In the coming weeks, as the story came together in the edit, a few things became clear. Firstly, warehouses make for great horror settings, and police officers are a pretty great starting point if you need a hero, a villain, or just someone likely to be poking their nose around in a dark warehouse.

Secondly, the eight-minute film we just made was nowhere near long enough to do the idea justice.

And so, even as the short film began screening

around the world at horror festivals, the longer version of *Off Duty* was born.

However, even as I started typing away at a full-length screenplay, I knew deep down that trying to get funding for a debut feature film would be nearly impossible. I had spent years making projects with whatever resources I had to hand, telling stories simply for the enjoyment of it - so I would be hard-pressed to persuade someone to hand over a large budget.

That's when I finally realised why I was making films in the first place – all I wanted was to tell a good story, and get that story out where an audience could enjoy it. As someone who believes that no room is complete without a generous sprinkling of books, the answer was obvious – in prose, I could get my story to readers around the world.

I would love to think that one day *Off Duty* will make its way back onto the big screen, this time in all its full-length glory. But right now, I couldn't be happier to finally have something of my own that I can stuff onto my groaning bookshelves.

I really hope you enjoy it.

For Sam

1

To say the house was silent would seem merely to suggest the absence of noise. The house wasn't without noises - the creak of old copper piping, the gentle drip of a tap that no longer tightened, the tiny sound of wind whistling through glazing that had seen better days.

But had there been an observer in this small, unassuming property, wedged between identikit houses in an unassuming road, they would surely say the house was silent.

Room after room lay still, the chaos of half-unpacked boxes and suitcases leading in a winding trail towards an open bedroom door. Moonlight stole through crooked blinds, ricocheting from the slats to land on the face of the single, sleeping occupant, who sprawled on the bed as untidily as her belongings.

The house's quiet soundtrack didn't stir her, and her gentle breathing added to the score as she slumbered peacefully amongst the mess.

Over so many small sounds, the wardrobe's softly opening door went unnoticed.

It brushed across the carpet, yawning wide, revealing the dark interior of the cupboard, where there was… nothing. No boxes had been unpacked into the tidy, empty space. No possessions sat on the shelves or hung from the rail. Nothing was inside the wardrobe. And after a long moment, Nothing left it.

Nothing stared down at the figure in the bed, who still slept peacefully, unaware of the door which now hung open only inches from her sleeping face. Nothing moved silently around the edge of the bed, getting closer and closer to the slight rise and fall of the crumpled duvet, closer and closer to the imperceptibly breathing face.

Then the house chimed in, with an uncharacteristically loud bang, perhaps a pipe, perhaps the whistling breeze catching something at just the right angle to topple it. Whatever the source, Nothing wanted to know about it.

Moving through the door, down the darkened hallway, slipping between boxes and cases, Nothing headed down the stairs, unlit by moonlight that spilled in a jagged, colourful pattern through the stained glass of the front door. It travelled around the corner of the stairs, past the empty nails where pictures once hung, past the kitchen, and on into the half-unpacked lounge.

On a low, old-fashioned coffee table, stained with years of loving use from former owners, sat a large, black kit bag, in such pristine condition that it practically gleamed in the moonlit living room. Its open zip revealed flashes of the cuffs, boots and vest nestled inside. Paper timetables and itineraries were stacked next to it, topped with a leather card holder.

The card holder itself lay open, proudly displaying a similarly pristine ID card, showing the slightly panicked face of PC Jess Layton, newly arrived member of the Huntshire Police Force. Her long brown hair and sporadically plucked eyebrows suggested that she might, in fact, be the untidy figure sleeping peacefully upstairs.

Without warning, the whole pile was swept violently from the coffee table, tumbling into a stack of jumbled boxes and sending a lamp crashing to the floor. As the silence in the house shattered, Jess Layton sat bolt upright in bed.

Stumbling groggily from her slumber, she burst out onto the landing and then stopped, listening intently to the seemingly empty house. The hair on her head was piled untidily from sleep, the hair on her arms stood on end. Taking a deep breath, she began to edge towards the stairs.

'Police!' Jess called in an unsteady voice, trying to sound braver than she looked in her baggy old pyjamas. She took a couple of gentle steps down the stairs, straining to hear a reaction. Nothing moved. As she reached the bottom of the stairs, she peered into the dark hallway, before groping for the light switch. Light flared into the darkness - but still nothing emerged.

Jess trod quietly towards the front door, peering through the patterned glass of the window. There didn't seem to be any sign of movement in the darkness beyond her quietly sheltered porch. As she stood there, squinting into the gloom, she heard the soft rustle of something shifting behind her.

Whirling around, Jess stared down the now lit hallway, towards the gaping door of the lounge. Clenching her fists, she began to edge towards it, feeling her heart beginning to race beneath the thin cotton of her pyjama top. Crossing the threshold, she flipped the light switch and raised her fists.

The lit room revealed nothing more than a mess of tumbled boxes and spilled possessions. Spotting her kit bag, Jess lunged forwards and reached inside, withdrawing a sleek metal baton. With her other hand she seized the leather badge holder, before racking the baton open with a crisp click, and drawing herself upright.

'We could be about to set a record for burglary response times here…' she called, struggling to keep her voice light. The room stayed still and silent.

Slowly, carefully, Jess travelled through the empty house, turning on every light and opening every door. Each window lock was carefully examined, every handle turned, the location of every key double-checked. No sign of any intruder could be found.

Eventually, as Jess stood framed in yet another empty cupboard doorway, she made an exasperated time check on her phone. The numbers seemed to mock her as she realised it was now 2:00am and every nerve in her body was still firing like she was about to run a hundred-metre dash.

As she stood, heart still pounding even in the bright, reassuring lights of her hallway, the silence was suddenly broken by a loud gurgle from Jess's empty stomach. It seemed her body wasn't too keen on skipping dinner after a hectic day of house moving, and then a full sweep of her new home to boot. Sighing, Jess left all the upstairs lights blazing and headed back down towards the quiet kitchen.

The polythene film covering a microwave meal for one took the brunt of Jess's feelings. After pounding it repeatedly with a fork, she wasn't sure it would be a particularly effective steam trap, but it definitely made her feel better.

As she slammed it into the microwave and started the timer, Jess hunted through a half-unpacked box to find a dusty wine glass. She gave it a rinse under the tap and pulled a cheap bottle of red wine from the small bag of groceries she had grabbed in the course of her chaotic house move.

The microwave whirred comfortingly, and Jess took a deep, steadying breath as she poured the wine. The first sip was sharp and acidic, but helped to calm her as she looked around the still unfamiliar kitchen. Her eyes travelled across the slightly chipped tiles, battered cupboards and scuffed floor, none of which were improved by the chaos of Jess's moving boxes. Taking her mind off mysterious late-night noises was definitely harder in a house that didn't yet feel like home.

Suddenly feeling the overwhelming need to hear other human voices, she reached out for the radio that perched on the kitchen side and flicked it on. It crackled into life with the artificially happy chatter of a local radio DJ.

'Hello, and welcome back to the late show with me, Ricky White - getting you through the night!' the radio trilled. 'In just a few minutes, we'll be asking you to tell us why you've had the world's greatest Monday, in a ground-breaking new segment called... Hashtag Humblebrag.'

Jess groaned slightly and rubbed her eyes.

'But first,' Ricky White added jovially, 'here's one for all you winners. This is the Black Dog Blues, enjoy it with your meal for one!'

Jess glowered at the radio and went to turn over the station. As she reached for the dial, the lights suddenly flickered, and the radio's feed distorted for a moment. The gentle background hum of the microwave seemed to be faltering. Confused, Jess turned to look at it, wondering whether the old appliance was overloading a circuit.

She turned the microwave off for a moment, and the lights and radio returned to normal. After a careful pause, she tried pushing the button to start cooking again. The lights and music held steady.

Shrugging, Jess polished off the remains of her glass while waiting for the meal to finish cooking. As the microwave chimed its successful conclusion, she poured herself another generous measure, before seizing the meal and retreating to the sofa next door.

The living room felt a little more comfortable to Jess. Despite being just as untidy as the rest of her house, it had one major advantage - this was where she had brought the squashy old sofa from her mother's home, the one she had spent many years playing, napping and watching TV on. There was a little groove in one cushion that she had come to think of as her particular place, worn smooth from years of being lounged upon.

It was this familiar spot that she now curled up in, wine on the coffee table in front of her, wolfing down the microwave meal directly from its plastic container. She kept the racked baton perched on the table next to her wine glass, only a single lunge away from her hand.

The rest of the living room still loomed strange around her, and Jess found herself huddling slightly into the crook of the sofa's arm, enjoying the sensation of the old worn fabric brushing against her skin. The shabby overhead lampshade cast odd shadows onto the hulking, dark piano that still stood against one wall, the relic of a former occupant who hadn't had the inclination to either tune it or haul it away across the worn carpet.

But as Jess shifted in her seat, she released the faintest whiff of her mother's old perfume, drifting softly out of the threadbare cushions. A slight smile twitched the corner of her mouth.

With the strains of music still chirping from the

radio next door, and a warm meal in her belly, Jess felt herself finally beginning to relax.

Then the lights flickered once and went out.

The radio fell silent in the next room, and Jess became acutely aware of her own breathing, suddenly loud and panicked in the dark. In the gloom, she reached out and clumsily set the meal down on the coffee table, picked up the baton, and made her way cautiously across the room, treading carefully around the forest of boxes.

Reaching the window, she cracked the blinds, allowing a small amount of moonlight to edge through into the darkness. After a hurried glance into the shadows now pooling in every corner, she peered out into her back garden, wondering if this was a sudden power cut.

Along the backs of the oblivious houses that lined her garden, Jess could see the golden glow of security lights, night lights spilling from bedroom windows, and the faint strains of someone's television as they sat up late into the warm summer night. For a moment, she lingered by the window, overcome with a sudden longing to be in one of those other houses - any house would do, it just needed to be full of people, noise and light, not this strange shell in an unfamiliar town.

Then she heard something behind her - a soft, gentle thump.

Jess whirled around. Her glass had fallen to the floor and was bleeding red wine all over the beige carpet. Instinctively, she lunged for it, as though to clean it up, and then hesitated. It didn't take a police officer to deduce that glasses didn't simply knock themselves over.

Trying to fight back a rising sense of panic, she peered into every corner of the dark room. Nothing was there.

Jess took a single step forwards – and a single, untuned note rang out from the piano.

She froze, as the echoes of the discordant sound faded away. Her eyes were glued to the brooding shape of the piano, squatting ominously in the dark. A shaft of moonlight spilled onto the keys, and they almost seemed to glow a little in the gloom.

In the dim light, Jess watched in horror as another key was pressed, and another, and another. Nothing was playing them.

It took a moment for Jess to realise that the sudden cry in the darkness had come from her own lips. As she began to run, she seized the black kit bag instinctively, and pelted for the door to the living room. As her feet thundered towards the hallway, the door ahead suddenly flew shut in front of her.

Jess staggered backwards as it slammed, then lunged instinctively for the handle, trying to push the door open, but it was stuck fast. She grappled with the metal of the handle, trying to wrestle it free, but it felt like something was gripping it hard from the other side.

Almost sobbing in frustration and fear, Jess pounded a fist against the door, but it wouldn't budge. She took a deep breath, stepped back, then hurled herself bodily at the wood.

The door finally whirled open, and Jess shot out into the moonlit hallway. She made it to the front door, scrabbling for her keys on the hallway table and thrusting them frantically into the lock. She turned backwards just in time to see the open lounge door fly shut again with a crash.

Without question, there couldn't be anyone else in the house.

With that thought churning through her mind, Jess yanked the front door open and bolted into the night, with nothing but her police kit, baton and old pyjamas. She flew down the path towards her car, jerking the door open before throwing herself inside and slamming it shut.

She disentangled herself clumsily, then sat for a long moment behind the wheel of her battered third-hand Peugeot, staring up at the house she was now too scared to live in alone. Tears prickled the corners of her eyes, before the feeling finally overcame her, and Jess began to sob.

*

One really good cry later, Jess wiped the smeared mascara from her cheeks, and pulled out her phone. She opened up her browser, fingers hovering over the touchscreen, wondering how best to phrase her rather unusual search.

'*What to do if my house is haunted,*' she began eventually, feeling a little foolish as she did so. The

amazon.co.uk®

A gift note from Rosemary Pantling:

Thought you might enjoy reading Becki's new book! Love from: Rosemary

Gift note included with **Off Duty (The Graveyard Shift Trilogy)**

search results all seemed to quickly draw the same conclusion as they rattled in, and she scrolled down the list of previewed pages.

Cleanse the house… not sure what to do? Call a psychic!

Go to a psychic… don't fuck about with the dead!

Try a psychic - can't put a price on a poltergeist-free home!

Is your house haunted? Try our psychic services! Our prices are spoooookily low…

Jess rolled her eyes a little at the last one, but then looked back up at the dark façade of her house. There was something about the way it innocently sat there, nestled in its neat little row of matching homes, that made the whole thing seem worse. No one else from the neighbourhood was sat out here in their pyjamas, with a baton nestling on their lap.

Sighing, she looked back down at the phone and tried another search.

'*Psychic Services in my area,*' she tried. To her tear-stained surprise, a highly-rated entry suggested she might like to call Leaford Psychic Services, whose great reviews promised such delights as '*quick response times*', '*reassuring service,*' and '*lovely cup of tea while I waited*'.

So she did.

2

'You look tired,' PC Jennifer Grant observed, giving Jess a cursory glance over her shoulder as she strode through the shabby hallways of the police station. Now dressed in her work boots, Jess stood a comfortable six feet tall, and could practically see clear over the top of PC Grant's diminutive head. Somehow, she still found herself hurrying to keep up, as she followed in the wake of the older officer's confident stride.

'I didn't sleep well,' Jess admitted, trying to take in the bewildering line of doorways as they travelled rapidly past.

'Sure, I didn't sleep well either before my first day here,' Grant admitted cheerfully, 'but I think that just helped me blend in. No one here ever gets any sleep. Well, unless they're on firearms, the lazy bastards.'

Her final comment was directed straight at two enormous officers who had emerged from a side room and were ambling down the narrow corridor towards them. They scowled good-naturedly at Grant, who pulled a face back.

'Yeah, you heard me up there,' she called up at their towering faces as they passed, and Jess blushed as the two huge officers looked her over passively.

'Are all firearms officers that massive?' she asked Grant quietly once she thought they were out of earshot.

'Oh yeah,' the older officer mused, 'not sure why they give them guns really, they could probably just sit on people. Here we are!'

Grant swung open a battered door, and without waiting for Jess, headed on through. Jess caught the door awkwardly on the backswing and edged inside. As she entered, three faces turned to stare at her.

The nearest face beamed genially from behind slightly wonky glasses. It belonged to a man in roughly his mid-thirties, who had somehow managed to get creases in his non-iron, police-issued shirt.

Behind him sat two women, who were sitting in perfect tandem, with their arms crossed and feet outstretched from their worn office chairs. They were otherwise each other's perfect opposite, one young, broad and muscular with a strikingly severe haircut topping a kindly face, the other older, tiny and almost delicate, except for her powerful scowl. Luckily this expression didn't seem especially directed at Jess, but instead displayed a general disdain for the room at large.

Grant, unperturbed, began gesturing around the office.

'Everyone, this is our new probationer, Jess Layton. This is Hunter,' she announced, as the scowling officer nodded curtly, 'Packer,' as the larger woman gave a friendly wave, 'and Einstein.'

The bespectacled officer pushed his glasses up his nose and smiled, as Jess raised her eyebrows.

'Not my real name,' he clarified, 'I got a question right on a pub quiz... once.'

Jess started in surprise as the door behind her banged open. She whirled around to find herself practically nose-to-nose with another officer, whose rumpled black hair was as untidy as Jess's bedroom. It was hard to place his age, as the faint lines around his mouth ran down into a tiny patch of stubble that looked like a much younger man's attempt at growing a beard. He stared blankly back at her from exhausted eyes.

'Ah,' Grant announced brightly, 'and this is your tutor. Danny, meet Jess.' Jess noticed the officer's eyes narrow as he looked her up and down, before grunting slightly.

'I'm PC Jackson. Nice to meet you,' he muttered, before walking past her and making a beeline for the tiny kitchenette in the corner of the office. Jess felt Grant emit a small sigh beside her, as her tutor began banging cupboard doors open in search of caffeine.

Her fellow officers watched Jess expectantly, and

after a moment's uncomfortable silence, she took a deep breath and stepped forwards.

'I'll do that!' she called, trying to match Grant's bright, cheerful tone. 'Would anyone like tea?'

Spurred on by the appreciative chorus of nods and murmurs of approval from her new colleagues, Jess headed towards PC Jackson's hunched figure, which was currently battling with the ancient kettle. He didn't look up as she arrived into the tiny kitchenette, so she hovered awkwardly for a moment, before trying a nervous cough. He whirled around, brandishing the limescale-covered appliance at her absent-mindedly.

'Really, I'm - I'm happy to do that if you want,' she offered again, and he shrugged.

'Fine. Grant made a chart. Our mugs are on the hooks, also Grant,' he sighed, before shuffling back towards the office. Jess grabbed the kettle as he passed her and set it carefully on its base, where it wobbled ominously. She tried flipping the button - nothing. For a moment, she considered asking for assistance from one of her new colleagues, and then thought about how it would look if the brand-new probationer asked how to turn on a kettle.

With a brief jiggle of the faulty appliance and a silent prayer, Jess flipped the switch again, and her sigh of relief was lost in the familiar bubble of heating water. Turning to look for mugs, she found that Grant had indeed added a cosy touch to the worn kitchenette with a little row of six hooks, over which a peeling yellow Post-it note declared that these mugs were '*Property of B Shift*'. Underneath, a second note invited A Shift to '*piss off and learn to load a fucking dishwasher*'. Jess grinned.

Sure enough, hanging right alongside the hooks was a comprehensive chart of caffeinated beverages, divided into a handy grid with instructions of which mug to use, and what to fill it with.

Jess began diving through cupboards, throwing tea bags and instant coffee into a mug that could be charitably described as a china bucket (Packer's), a faded, floral-print cup (Grant's), a spotlessly clean mug decorated with a mildly grumpy portrait of the Queen (Hunter's), and a slightly chipped mug that invited the reader to 'Fuck the police… we come with handcuffs,' (Einstein's). PC Jackson's mug turned out to be plain, blue, and destined to be filled with only strong, black coffee.

She added milk and sugar as per the sheet's explicit instructions, then began distributing mugs around the office. Hunter sniffed hers suspiciously as she received it, and then took a cautious sip, before turning to Jess with an expression remarkably like that of the Queen emblazoned on her mug.

'You make shit tea,' she announced, shaking her head as she took another swig.

'Hunter!' Grant admonished her, before gingerly tasting her own and wincing.

'How can you make shit tea?' Packer wondered, gazing down at her mug in mild horror.

'It's okay, I prefer coffee anyway,' Einstein said happily, winking at Jess as he slurped his drink. He grimaced and wrinkled his nose. 'Wow, what did you do to that kettle?'

Dismayed, Jess returned to the list and found one final entry - requesting that black coffee be made for Sergeant Davies, in the 'big black mug'.

Jess poked her head out of the kitchenette and caught Einstein's eye.

'Um, Einstein?' she asked, 'is there a mug for the Sergeant?'

'Oh yeah,' he nodded, 'just too massive for the hooks. It's in the cupboard above the sink, can't miss it.'

Jess peeked into the suggested cupboard and lifted out the large black mug that loomed amongst the other assorted china. She threw in a teabag and began to pour, before realising in bemusement that the mug had been coated in colour-changing black paint, which was slowly dissolving away to reveal a lurid unicorn motif.

Grinning, Jess turned around and found herself staring at an enormous male chest, whose owner had entered the kitchenette quite silently. She looked upwards, eventually finding the face of the largest police officer she had ever seen.

Sergeant Davies gazed down at Jess, and noticed the mug clutched in her hands.

'Ah, that must be my coffee,' he rumbled genially, 'and you must be PC Layton. Hello.'

Jess glanced down and noticed the teabag now slowly sinking into the cup with silent horror, as the Sergeant took the mug gently from her protesting hands and glided silently back across the office. As Jess gazed after him, Grant slipped into the kitchenette, trying to subtly pour the remains of her tea into the sink.

'Time for briefing!' Grant announced, before striding back into the office, with Jess hurrying along after her. The rest of the shift fell into step with them. As they headed out through the door, Jess turned to Einstein.

'Einstein?'

'Yes, Jess?'

'Did Sergeant Davies used to be in firearms?'

'Yeah, he did. Why?'

'I dunno, just a hunch.'

The door swung shut behind them, and the office returned to comfortable silence, the smell of badly brewed tea still lingering in the air.

*

'VG, Sierra Romeo 2 5, I've got a domestic on an immediate at 3 Foxgloves Avenue. Two parties heard screaming down the line.'

A mere two minutes after their briefing ended, Jess found herself hurrying down the corridors once more, this time in the wake of PC Jackson's now caffeinated stride. Behind them, the rest of B Shift were heading back towards the office.

'Sierra Romeo 2 5, received,' Jackson muttered into his radio as he powered through the halls.

'Is it always like this?' Jess asked apprehensively,

slightly breathless with her efforts to keep up.

'Yeah, brace yourself, looks like you're off to a fun start!' Einstein called after her.

'Huh. I thought starting on a Tuesday would be quiet,' she mused, and B shift instantly broke into a chorus of groans. Even her tutor stopped and turned back, looking mildly horrified.

'Oh no, you never say that word...' Packer breathed.

'What word?' Jess asked, bewildered.

'Anytime someone says it's... "Q",' Packer explained, bringing her finger to her lips in a mock charade, 'is when everything goes to hell.'

A moment later, the corridor was filled with the buzz and crackle of radios, as the control room began frantically conveying calls. With much eye rolling and muttering, B Shift started falling in behind PC Jackson, who was once again grimly striding ahead.

Jess fell into the centre of the pack, carried along by a tide of uniformed officers. They burst out together into the bright morning, and Jess finally got to discover what her new job had in store.

*

Eight hours later, covered in bruises, dust and what Jess still sincerely hoped was mud, she half-collapsed back through the door of the office. The rest of her shift were packing up, stretching bruised limbs and massaging stiff shoulders.

21

Jess hovered nervously beside a weary PC Jackson, wondering what the protocol was at the end of such a busy day. Seeing Jess arrive in the doorway, Packer looked up and grinned.

'Here she is!' she cried gleefully, 'star of the radio channels. Go on then, Jackson, what the fuck happened to you two out there?'

Her tutor muttered something darkly before disappearing once again towards the kitchenette. Jess stood frozen, feeling a blush slowly spread across her cheeks. Packer strode over and clapped her on the shoulder.

'Layton, my lovely, did they teach you about the Cake Act in training school?' she boomed genially.

'Um, they did mention it…'

'Excellent! Essentially, it's a very, very important piece of legislation, determining exactly when you should supply your fellow officers with delicious cake for a variety of offences. Let me read you your count today, I think it's a fucking record,' Packer hooted, moving over to a piece of A4 paper stuck neatly on to a noticeboard on one side of the room.

As Jess followed her, she noticed the paper had been at first carefully typed, but then amended generously over the years by a variety of scrawling hands.

Cake Act 2011

(As Amended by the Cake Offences Schedule 2016)

Officers of the Huntshire Police Force will be issued with a Cake Fine for the following offences (payment will be greater than or equal to one doughnut per shift colleague)

Sec. 1 - Late Cakes

Sec. 2 - Crash (job vehicle) Cakes

Sec. 3 - Birthday Cakes

Sec. 4 - Emergency Button (false activation of) Cakes

Sec. 5 - Emergency Button (genuine activation of, but lacking hospitalisation) Cakes

Sec. 6 - Unlawful Arrest Cakes

Sec. 7 - Leaving Cakes

Sec. 8 - Joining Cakes

Sec. 9 - Married/Divorced/Engaged Cakes

Sec. 10 - Stinger Deployment Cakes

Sec. 11 - Peer (Majority) Decision Cakes

Sec. 12 - Escapee Cakes

Sec. 13 - Saving of Life Cakes

Sec. 14 - First Arrest Cakes

Sec. 15 - Serious Arrest Cakes (murder or dangerous driving and attempts of such)

Sec. 16 - CS Gas Deployment Cakes (cheesecake level if on colleagues)

Sec. 17 - Losing Equipment Cakes

Sec. 18 – Late Provision of Cakes, Cakes

Sec. 19 - Amending the Cake Act Cakes

'Right then!' Packer called happily, 'according to the radio, you managed the following… starting off with a clean Section Two, clipped the police car on a wall. While exiting the car park. That's cakes!'

'Followed up,' chimed in Einstein, looking up from his desk, 'with an outstanding combination of Sections Four, Five, Fourteen and Fifteen - while making your first arrest on a GBH suspect, got trigger happy with your panic button and called us all whizzing to your aid while he was barely pissed off. Then managed to wind him up so much you got in a massive barney, triggering emergency button push number two. Legitimate - but no hospital, sorry mate!'

'Not to mention,' came the dry drawl of Hunter from the corner of the office, 'hearing the immortal words come chiming over the radio – "suspect on foot. I'm in pursuit. He's 5'10, early twenties, medium build, and…" '

The other officers joined in gleefully as she spoke.

'…wearing handcuffs on one wrist!'

'That's a Twelve I'm afraid love, and a Seventeen for the lost cuffs,' sighed Grant, clapping Jess sympathetically on the shoulder.

'Also,' added Packer hopefully, 'there's Section Eight… did you already bring your Joining Cakes?'

Jess shook her head sorrowfully.

'Section Eighteen! More cakes!' cried the office happily, before starting to peel away into their own conversations, leaving a dejected Jess still standing awkwardly in the doorway.

Throughout the exchange, she had noticed PC Jackson wincing with each fresh memory of their shift together. It certainly hadn't been her idea of a fantastic first impression - and she was acutely aware that the other officers only knew what had been reported over the radio.

Between messing up the reading of the caution, failing to cuff multiple suspects, and generally seeming to get on the wrong side of every Huntshire citizen she interacted with, Jess was fairly sure she had to be one of the worst probationers her shift had ever seen. At least, as a freshly arrived Huntshire citizen herself, she fervently hoped so.

Just then, the door to the office banged open again, and in strode five officers. Even in the dull black uniform of the Huntshire Police Force, they stood resplendent and alert, clearly no strangers to either a gym or a tanning salon.

'Evening, B Shift,' called the officer at the front of the gleaming pack. His hair was so expertly coiffed that Jess's own tousled, grubby mane practically shrank in its presence. The man's uniform marked him out as a sergeant, but his manner suggested that he considered himself far above that.

She heard Jackson give an irritated exhale as he arrived beside her.

'Evening, A Shift,' rumbled Sergeant Davies, appearing silently behind them. He swept the leading officer to one side, beginning to brief him.

The rest of the newly arrived shift moved into the office, finding their desks. One stunningly blonde woman was making a big show of dusting off Einstein's chair before sitting down, while an astonishingly muscular constable did stretches next to Jess's recently vacated desk before deigning to seat himself.

'So, this is A Shift,' announced Einstein cheerfully, appearing at Jess's elbow. 'Absolute bunch of pricks, but at least they do our paperwork after we've done the hard bits.'

The immaculately turned out officers pretended not to hear him.

'What do we do?' Jess asked PC Jackson nervously as the shift handover continued around them. He shrugged, looking exhausted.

'Just pack up your things and go home, I guess.'

He shuffled off towards his desk, and Jess began to edge awkwardly towards the door.

'How many cakes should I bring tomorrow?' she asked Packer, as the large woman strode happily past her, heading for freedom.

'Put it this way, I'd use a trolley, not a basket. See you tomorrow!' she called, laughing. Hunter followed her, grunting a goodbye.

Einstein held the door kindly for her as Jess walked through, feeling dejected.

'Everyone struggles on their first day,' he reassured her, 'we were all shit to start with. I was with Sergeant Davies on my very first call - I ducked a punch and he ended up getting a black eye,' he confided, after checking the massive bulk of the Sergeant was nowhere to be seen.

'Really?' Jess asked, feeling slightly better.

'Yeah. He slammed the guy through a wardrobe straight after though. Absolutely epic,' Einstein sighed.

Patting her pockets, Jess suddenly realised she was missing her warrant card. Fearing another cake fine coming on, she turned back for the door.

'I'll catch up with you,' she told Einstein, hurrying back towards the office.

As she began to push open the door, she heard the voices of PC Jackson and PC Grant coming from the other side. She hesitated, not particularly wanting to see her unimpressed mentor again before the end of her shift - and then held the door slightly ajar as she heard her own name mentioned.

'Layton is quite honestly the worst fucking officer I have ever seen. I refuse to believe this is normal for a recruit,' Jackson was stating bluntly. Despite her low expectations, his voice felt like a punch to her guts, which were still aching from her encounter with the angry GBH suspect many hours ago.

'Just be patient,' Grant pleaded, 'I know she's your first tutee, but we've seen this before. She'll do a few weeks, fail to pass, and then get a job in force control room or something. That's just the way it goes sometimes. Don't take it personally.'

Somehow, hearing it in Grant's friendly tones was so much worse. On the other side of the door,

Jess took a deep breath and pushed it open.

The two officers on the other side stared at her for a moment, and then Grant rearranged her face hurriedly into a sympathetic grin. Jackson didn't bother.

'Jess!' Grant cried over-enthusiastically. 'Can we help you?'

'Forgot my card,' Jess muttered.

Her face reddening under the A Shift's curious glances, Jess swept up the forgotten warrant card from her desk and shuffled back towards the door. As she passed her mentor, she looked up at him, silently pleading for some sign of empathy.

'Good night,' she offered quietly. The sentiment was returned by Grant, while Jackson remained completely unmoved.

Jess pushed the door hard, striding out into the corridor, hoping neither officer had noticed how hard she was trying to keep her eyes dry.

*

Later that evening, still dressed in her work uniform with an old hooded sweatshirt thrown hastily over the top, Jess pulled her car into a quiet residential street. As the vehicle pulled to a stop underneath a softly glowing streetlight, the phone in her pocket pinged quietly.

'Don't forget - you're due for your FREE consultation with Leaford Psychic Services!' a message announced cheerfully. Jess took a deep breath and peered into

the dark street, trying to make out the house numbers.

Her phone chimed again, continually ringing this time, and Jess's stomach dropped a little as she looked down at the screen. The picture on display was of a beaming, middle-aged woman, who had clearly taken the image herself while positioned just a little too close to the lens. Jess didn't need to read the name displayed above it before she took a deep breath and picked up the video call.

'Hi, Mum,' Jess said, quickly rearranging her face into a tired smile. As the picture flicked into life on the screen, her mother's image was replaced by a moving version of the same beaming, lined face, once again just a touch too close to the camera.

'Jess!' Alex Layton cried happily, peering up at her daughter, her eyes searching for evidence of a good night's sleep and a nutritious meal or two. 'How was your first day?'

'It was great, Mum, really good,' Jess assured her, but her mother frowned back from the tiny screen.

'Is everyone nice? Do you like it?'

'It's just been one day, Mum, but yeah, it's fine,' Jess insisted, and Alex sighed.

'How is the house? Is everything unpacked yet?' she asked, eyes roving again, clearly taking in the car that Jess was still sat in. 'Have you only just got home? Are you doing extra time already?'

'No, Mum, I just have errands to run on the way back. House is great, not unpacked yet, but I'll send you pictures, OK?' Jess mumbled, glancing at the clock on her car's dashboard and realising she was about to be late to her appointment.

'OK. Sorry honey, I know you're busy. But you can call whenever you need me, alright? And I'll come any time, or you can come back home…'

'Mum, look, it's really sweet but it's a two-and-a-half-hour drive. Why don't I call you when I've done my first full shift rotation, I can tell you about it then, and I'll show you the house on video chat, OK?'

'OK, honey. I love you,' Alex told her, and as her eyebrows scrunched up with a mix of pride and worry, she looked remarkably like Jess. 'I'm really proud of you. I just wish they'd been recruiting closer –'

'Mum, we've been over this,' Jess sighed. 'Look, I need to go. I – I promise I'll call soon, alright?'

'Alright. OK. Love you,' Alex sighed, and Jess gave her another tired smile.

'I love you too. Bye, Mum,' Jess told her firmly, and shut off the call. She sat back for a moment in her seat, closing her eyes and taking another long, slow breath. Then she stuffed her phone back into her pocket and clambered out of her car, checking that her kit was stowed safely out of sight, before beginning to walk cautiously up the road.

As she moved through patches of darkness between the streetlights, Jess found herself instinctively looking over her shoulder, drawing her arms around herself in the big, comfortable sweatshirt. There didn't seem to be anyone else around, and the windows of the houses that stared out onto the road were all covered by thick, luxurious curtains.

Eventually, Jess found herself standing in front of a diminutive bungalow. The house nestled innocuously amongst its showier mock-Tudor neighbours, its garden overgrown with riotous wildflowers that gave off a heavenly scent in the evening air. Jess breathed it in deeply as she stood in front of the door, before reaching up to ring the heavy metal doorbell.

The bell jangled inside the hallway with a dull echo, and a light suddenly flared through a small, densely patterned window that was set into the top half of the smartly painted front door. As Jess peered through it, she could see a shadowy figure approaching down the hall.

She heard the figure's steps come to a shuffling halt as it reached the door, and there came the creaking sound of an old lock, followed by the sliding click of a bolt, and then another bolt, and another. Finally, the door swung slowly inwards and Jess's mouth fell open.

There in the doorway, sporting a distinctive mop of untidy black hair and an unfortunately familiar scowl, stood PC Jackson.

3

As it turned out, there was still a lovely cup of tea on offer. Jess sipped it gratefully as she sat awkwardly on a spindly wooden chair, perched beside a round table whose lovingly polished top was covered with an elaborate crocheted tablecloth. The room around her was almost exactly what she had expected – elegant silk drapes, shelves piled with mysterious objects and ornaments, and atmospherically dim lamps covered in heavy red shades.

The company, however, was significantly less expected.

PC Jackson sat opposite her, considering her carefully over his own cup of tea. After several uncomfortable sips, Jess decided it was time to break the silence.

'So… is this what you do when you're off duty?'

Jackson sighed and set down his cup.

'It's my grandmother's business, but I help her out on the side. It's technically a two-person job... I just offered to do some consultation appointments while she's taking time off.'

'Oh no, is she OK?' Jess asked, also setting down her tea.

'Yeah, yeah - on yet another cruise,' he sighed, glancing over to a photograph balanced precariously on a haphazardly piled shelf.

Peering over, Jess could see a tall, glamorous woman beaming out of the picture frame, posing in what appeared to be the dining room of a cruise ship. She was surrounded, for some reason, by much younger women dressed in elaborate carnival outfits, full of feathers, bright colours and jewels. PC Jackson's grandmother, however, was somehow managing to outdo them all with a feather boa practically as large as she was, a stunning scarlet gown and lipstick to match. Jess liked her already.

Glancing back up, she noticed that Jackson was still watching her levelly.

'You don't seem that surprised to see me,' she observed, and he shrugged.

'Recognised the name from your appointment. I guessed it was probably you.'

'Right. So... what exactly is it that you do?' she asked cautiously.

'Well, generally what we advertise,' he sighed. 'We advise people on supernatural matters, communicate with spirits, and... intervene, if necessary.'

'Okay,' Jess offered helplessly, feeling as though

her brain was struggling to process this unprecedented social situation.

'You know,' she offered eventually, trying to achieve a light conversational tone, 'I always thought psychic also meant… predicting the future and things. Like tarot cards?'

'Yes,' Jackson snapped, 'I know. My grandmother and I discussed whether the business would be better labelled as "mediums" rather than psychic… but she felt psychic would be better for Google rankings.'

Jess grinned.

'I guess I found you, so maybe she has a point?'

'Hmmm.'

'So how does this work?' Jess asked, looking around the cluttered room, half expecting to see a Ouija board poking out from behind a lamp or a pile of old books. Jackson continued to study her for a moment, before taking a deep breath.

'Look, Jess… I don't know about this,' he began awkwardly, 'I really didn't know whether to take this appointment.'

They sat together for a long moment, watching each other carefully. Then Jess took a deep breath and spoke.

'I know you're not exactly my biggest fan,' she admitted, 'and I can understand why. But I need you to appreciate that what you saw today was me… after seeing what I'm fairly sure was a ghost. In my house.'

'You *saw* a ghost?' Jackson asked sharply, and

Jess hesitated.

'Well, I didn't technically *see* it. But I saw what it was doing... does that make sense?'

Jackson nodded slowly.

'It does. That's one of the ways I like to check... whether a sighting is real or not.'

'Sorry?'

'It's not possible for a human being to see spirits with the naked eye,' Jackson continued, and Jess was struck by the sincerity in his voice as he leaned forwards slightly, bringing his face further into the golden lamplight. He seemed a little younger out of his uniform, closer to Jess's own mid-twenties.

'But... can *you* see them?' Jess asked pointedly, and for a second, a smile flicked over PC Jackson's face.

'So just to be clear, you're comfortable with the idea that spirits exist?' he continued hesitantly, and Jess realised his fingers were tapping tensely against his knee. She nodded slowly, noticing that the tiny smile was still twitching at the corner of his mouth. Making her tutor happy was definitely not a familiar feeling, and she found herself relaxing slightly.

'I wouldn't - I mean, I didn't used to think it made much sense. But last night... I know what I saw, and there's no way there was another human being in my house.'

'Alright. So, let's start off with what you saw,' Jackson offered, and his nervous finger-tapping stopped as he frowned in concentration at Jess. She

felt herself leaning in too, feeling almost conspira-
torial as they huddled together in the dim lamplight.

'So last night, I'd just finished moving all my stuff
in and gone to bed, when I was woken up by -
something, I'm not entirely sure what. I just heard a
noise, and a load of my things had been disturbed
downstairs, but everything was locked up tight, and
there wasn't any obvious intruder.'

'Sure.'

'Then... well, I was sat in my living room, and all
the lights went out.'

'Interesting,' Jackson nodded. 'Turned off at the
switch?'

'No... it was like a power cut. Everything in the
house went off.'

'Unusual... OK, what happened next?'

'Erm, the piano started playing by itself, and I -
well, I pegged it to be honest,' Jess admitted sheep-
ishly. 'Then it was like something was trying to trap
me in the lounge... but I got out the front door, and,
er, spent the rest of the night in the car.'

Jackson nodded thoughtfully again.

'Have you been back since?' he asked, and Jess
shook her head.

'No... I thought showering at the police station
might be a better idea,' she admitted, and to her
surprise, her tutor grinned at her.

'Don't blame you. It sounds like it's quite a
poltergeist you've got there. It's going to be a short
wait though, I'm afraid,' he mused, and Jess's face
fell.

'I mean, I'm happy to pay more if there's any way of rushing it?' she offered awkwardly, but Jackson shook his head.

'It's not that. This is a two-person job I'm afraid, Jess, and my grandmother's not back for another fortnight.'

He sat back in his chair, rubbing his temples thoughtfully, as Jess sank down in her own seat, thinking dejectedly of two potential weeks spent sleeping in her cramped car.

'I mean… if you need another pair of hands, maybe I could help?' she offered, but her tutor shook his head, sighing.

'I really don't know about that, Jess, we don't really discuss the details of what we do with… outsiders. You'll need to wait until I've got another trained professional with me before we can get this done. Why don't I let you know when my grand-mother's back, and we can set a date from there?' Jackson sighed, and drained the last of his tea, watching Jess carefully over the lip of his mug.

'Right,' she agreed, trying frantically to think of anything that might change his mind. 'Just a thought though… I mean, I am security vetted.'

'Sorry?' her tutor asked, looking bemused.

'Well, I had to be security vetted to get into the police, so if your process is a secret, no problem. You can trust me,' Jess gabbled, as Jackson raised his eyebrows at her.

'Hmm. That's not really -'

'And anyway, you're going to have to put up

with tutoring me for the next ten weeks regardless, and I'll be better at my job if I'm not sleeping in a car,' Jess continued. Jackson's face clouded, and Jess's babble ground to a halt.

For a long moment, he stared at her across the table, as her anxiously knotting eyebrows pleaded over at his own deep scowl.

'Jess, in the nicest possible way, are you telling me that if we banished your poltergeist, you would instantly become a better police officer?' he asked eventually.

'Well… you've never actually seen me be a police officer without a poltergeist problem, so I guess… you don't have any evidence to suggest otherwise?' she tried, and to her relief, saw his smile twitching back into life. 'I promise, I'll do whatever you tell me to do,' she continued, and her tutor nodded slowly.

'You know, this isn't exactly the usual way people begin doing this. We could both get into a lot of trouble,' he warned, but Jess felt her heart lift as she saw his frown dissolving. 'But if it's an emergency, and I can trust you, maybe we can work something out.'

Jess nodded eagerly. Jackson grunted resignedly and stood up, walking carefully around the small, cluttered room.

'Right. First things first, there's no equivalent of training college for this. You learn pretty much on the job, straight away,' he told her sternly, as he moved over to a crowded set of shelves. Old books, statuettes and picture frames clustered enticingly on every surface, but there was only one small pile that Jackson now reached for.

'So. In order to understand what we're dealing with, you need to know what a ghost fundamentally is,' he began, setting down the pile on the crocheted tablecloth.

A small, dark wooden chest came first, latched with a neat clasp that looked well-worn with use. Next to the box, he placed a pair of black tactical gloves and an old-looking leather scabbard with the hilt of a dagger poking out of the top.

Jess looked from the strange objects to her tutor, who was watching her curiously. She tried to remain nonchalant as her mind raced, wondering what purpose a pair of psychics might need tactical gloves and a dagger for.

'A ghost,' Jackson continued, sitting back down opposite Jess, 'is actually the part of you which resides on another plane, that's different to the one we're currently perceiving.'

'Another plane?' she asked, and noticed her tutor frown slightly again at the interruption. She bit her lip apologetically, and he took a deep breath before continuing.

'There are plenty of things that exist around us in ways we can't currently see or experience - but they're still present, and affecting everything we do. Your spirit, technically, is one of them. Currently, you're using it to control your body, so it experiences everything that your body does.'

Jackson suddenly reached out across the small

dining table and took one of Jess's hands. Surprised, she awkwardly allowed him to turn it over and gently run his fingers over her palm. She felt her face get a little hot as he watched her, and looked down at their hands, noticing how much larger his were than her own.

'You're feeling this sensation because something is touching your body, triggering nerve endings, and right now your spirit is in the right place to feel those nerve endings fire. But what if your spirit left your body?' he asked, and Jess looked back up at him, curious.

'So, is that astral projection?' she asked, and he smiled properly this time.

'Very good, Jess,' he said warmly, and she felt a gentle flush of pride. 'Outside of your body, you can perceive the plane your spirit exists on. You can still see everything here, but you can also see other spirits that are currently outside of their bodies. Some may be projecting like you are, and others are those who got stuck when their bodies died.'

Jackson's tone was matter-of-fact, but Jess still felt faint goose pimples prickle her neck.

'Stuck?' she asked quietly, and he nodded.

'Most spirits simply seem to disappear at the point a body dies. We don't know where they go, no one's ever managed to come back from whatever form of existence that might be. The only ones we know about are the very few that get stuck on the astral plane. And they,' he continued, gently opening the dark wooden chest, 'are the ones we have to deal with.'

As the heavy lid was lifted, it revealed a tightly packed tray of tiny bottles. Jackson removed one carefully, and Jess stared at the contents. A small amount of thick liquid was contained within, glinting a cold greenish-silver colour, despite the warm yellow light in the room.

'One sip of this, and you'll be able to walk around independently, as your spirit,' her tutor said softly, also gazing at the small bottle. 'The principle is surprisingly simple. It's a careful blend featuring tiny amounts of sage and silver, a recipe perfected over many generations. Spirits, sage and silver don't mix well, and putting this into your bloodstream is just enough to knock your soul sideways - and out.'

He grinned at her, and Jess was slightly surprised by his enthusiasm. Clearly, this was where her tutor had chosen to dedicate most of his energy. Despite herself, she could start to see why. If half of what PC Jackson had told her was true, she would certainly choose perceiving life on a whole other plane over fighting drunk drivers in a car park.

'Now, speaking of sage and silver - you know you won't be able to use your handcuffs for this,' Jackson continued, getting up again and rummaging in a nearby cupboard. He produced a large, finely woven net, which glinted faintly in the soft lamplight, and it pooled gently onto the table as he dropped it triumphantly.

'The fibres are made with a very similar blend of ingredients. Ghosts can't pass through it, and it causes an unpleasant sensation not unlike an electric shock. You'll need to get familiar with using it, that's going to be part of your job,' he told her, and Jess stared at him in surprise.

'I have to catch people - I mean, ghosts - in nets?' she asked, and he nodded, grinning. 'Well, I guess it's probably easier than handcuffs,' she muttered, and Jackson raised his eyebrows wryly.

'Why are you trusting me with this?' she asked suddenly, and he frowned at her.

'Your role in this is going to be simple to start with. You should be able to manage,' he replied shortly, and Jess blushed. 'You'll begin by keeping an eye on my body, while I project.'

'Why would I -' Jess began, but Jackson cut her off.

'If you're leaving behind an empty shell, you don't want to have any... unexpected guests in it,' he explained, and Jess felt a slight shiver pass through her. 'So. I'll tell you a password, and only you will know it. You always ask me for that word when I wake up. And if it's not me... it's your job to get whatever it is, back out.'

'Wait, what...' Jess started, as her tutor raised the small glass bottle again.

'A little of this normally does the trick,' he told her, smiling slightly. Jess nodded distractedly as she gazed at the swirling liquid inside the bottle, then frowned.

'So, if we can't see ghosts until we project,' she began slowly, 'then there could theoretically be one in the room when you tell me the password?'

'Not when we're here, thanks to all the sage and silver,' Jackson replied, smiling triumphantly, and Jess whipped around to survey the room they sat in, suddenly expecting to see heavy silver and green symbols nailed to every wall. 'It's in the window frames, it's in the floors, washed into the wallpaper paste, and even in those bloody bead curtains my grandmother's hung everywhere. While the execution was difficult, the principle really is that simple,' he finished, grinning at Jess's look of consternation.

'Alright. I think I'm getting it,' she said slowly, as her eyes caught the dagger, still sitting ominously on the tablecloth between them.

'What's that for?' she asked, and Jackson nodded approvingly, reaching for the tactical gloves. He pulled them on carefully, flexing his fingers inside the thick layers of slash-proof Kevlar and leather.

'This is what we need, for banishing a ghost,' he stated bluntly.

'Banish… so is that what we're going to do to my poltergeist?' Jess asked, her eyes narrowing as she watched the dagger guardedly.

'Mmm. Hopefully,' Jackson replied, reaching for the scabbard and drawing out the blade inside.

There was something indefinably old about the dagger, despite it looking wickedly sharp. Perhaps it was the dull sheen of the metal, which looked dark and smoky as though it had been beaten and folded many times to form the long, slightly curving blade. Maybe it was the way the handle had been elegantly carved with a twisting, almost organic-looking pattern, which sprouted smoothly upwards into the two long, reaching fingers of the cross-guard.

But there was nothing traditional about the tip.

The point of the dagger had been coated in something that caught the light softly, and shone a sinister, milky hue that stood out harshly against the darker metal beneath. Jess had never seen anything quite like it.

'What is that?' she asked quietly, staring transfixed at the dagger.

'Well, the blade is an alloy, mixed unsurprisingly with our old friend silver. When thrust with force, it can therefore 'pierce' a ghost. The coating on the tip, however… that's something quite special. It's a form of opiate, distilled from poppies, and carefully crafted over many generations to be one of the most lethal substances ever created,' Jackson told her quietly, as Jess continued to gaze at the point of the dagger. The painted coating seemed to shimmer subtly in the light.

'Never handle this blade without gloves, Jess. You remember your police training about never touching a white powder, just in case it's Fentanyl? Welcome to its much more dangerous cousin. Touch the coating on this, and it'll definitely kill you. Because not only will it race through your bloodstream and mess up your physical body, it also has the fun effect of instantly dissipating your spirit.'

For a moment, Jess could have sworn the tip of the blade almost glowed. Then Jackson slipped it back into its sheath and laid it on the table, before pulling off the gloves. Jess couldn't help but stare at the leather scabbard, trying not to shiver as she did so.

'Right. But we don't actually know where ghosts go, after that happens?' she asked, finally wrenching her eyes away.

'Sorry?' Jackson frowned, seeming a little surprised. 'What do you mean?'

Jess frowned back at him in the dim glow of the lamplit room, feeling strangely chilly despite the cosy surroundings.

'I mean, essentially you *kill* ghosts?' she asked quietly, and this time it was PC Jackson's eyebrows that shot towards the ceiling.

'Well, that's quite an existential question for someone who literally discovered their existence twenty-four hours ago,' he said pointedly, as Jess shifted uncomfortably in her chair. 'What exactly would you like me to do with them instead?'

'I don't know,' Jess replied helplessly, 'can't we… just catch them? I mean, think about it, when we need to stop a criminal, we don't just kill them.'

'Theoretically, you're correct,' Jackson agreed dryly, 'but you do appreciate that there isn't exactly an equivalent of prison for the undead, Jess. As I said, you can't just handcuff a ghost.'

'Right,' she agreed slowly, but continued to frown at the dagger. Her tutor sighed, seeming irritated.

'Look. If you're not comfortable with this, then I

think we'll leave this here. We've discussed this enough already. When my grandmother gets back, you can decide whether to use our services. Or not.'

He stood up from his chair, picking up their empty mugs. Jess looked up at him, dismayed.

'I didn't mean any offence, I just don't really understand it,' she began helplessly.

'Exactly,' Jackson responded firmly, his familiar scowl back in place. 'I shouldn't have - I mean, look, this is a complicated field, it's both public-facing and secretive, and morally messy. So why don't we leave this here, and you can concentrate on navigating all of that in your day job?'

Jess nodded slowly, and her tutor turned to take their cups into the kitchen, leaving her staring thoughtfully at the strange pile of objects that lay on the crocheted tablecloth.

*

After an awkward goodbye, Jess headed back out of the bungalow, and clambered into her car. As she looked out into the deserted road, she went to turn the key in the ignition, before slowly dropping her hand and chewing her lip. The thought of going back to sit outside her deserted house felt pretty unappealing, and this quiet street seemed empty enough to allow a small blue Peugeot to spend the night parked on it.

Sighing, Jess climbed out of the vehicle, and got into the back seat, where she curled up into the soft warmth of her sweatshirt. Her emergency blanket was still crumpled there after her previous night in the car, so she pulled it up over her, and clicked the car key to lock herself safely inside.

As she did so, the car's internal lights switched off, and she snuggled down into the darkness, trying to find a comfortable position to sleep. She closed her eyes against the golden glow of the nearest streetlight as it spilled through the rear windows of the car.

Suddenly, something knocked loudly against the glass, and Jess's eyes flew open. She scrambled upright, heart pounding as she turned to look for the source of the noise.

Stood outside the car, frowning in through the window, was PC Jackson. Jess instinctively reached out and wound the window down.

'Jess, are you really going to sleep out here?' he sighed, and she blushed.

'Sorry, I can move the car back to my road, I didn't mean to… sorry,' she babbled, and he shook his head despairingly.

'Why don't you just go to a hotel?'

'I, um, I don't really have the money right now,' Jess admitted awkwardly. 'The move cleaned me out, and we're not paid for another two weeks. It's pretty much car or poltergeist.'

Jackson took a deep breath and nodded slowly.

'Right, come on. I've got a sofa no one's using, you're not sleeping in your car,' he muttered, and Jess began to scramble eagerly out of the back seat as he turned towards the bungalow. As he began to move down the road, she hesitated, and he turned back to look at her.

'Look, it's fine, I'm a police officer for fuck's sake, not a serial killer,' he sighed irritably.

'Which would be a good cover for a serial killer,' Jess joked instinctively, and the corner of Jackson's mouth twitched again.

'Tell you what, I'll even make you a brew in the morning. Mostly because I think yours will actually kill me,' he muttered, as Jess began to grab her kit from the boot of the car, following her tutor gratefully down the dark, quiet street.

4

'So. If you're astrally projecting, can you walk through walls?' Jess asked eagerly the next morning, as PC Jackson's battered old Ford Fiesta pulled into the multistorey car park outside the police station.

'Yes,' he sighed, turning off the engine, which died with a faint splutter.

'Right. And can you also pick things up and throw them around, like a poltergeist can?' Jess mused, and her tutor grunted his assent. 'But how does that work? I mean, how can you both walk through a solid wall, and pick up a solid object?'

PC Jackson groaned and rubbed his eyes. Jess was feeling surprisingly refreshed after her night in the cosy, softly sage-scented bungalow, but the bags under her tutor's eyes seemed to have grown even deeper.

'Jess, this is exactly why astral projection normally takes years of training. You are literally talking about navigating a plane of existence you've never even been able to consciously perceive before, and then learning how to interact with this one at the same time… You know what, I've had nowhere near enough caffeine for this conversation,' Jackson grumbled, as he climbed out of the car.

Jess scrambled out after him, carefully balancing a stack of baked goods for her colleagues that would have clogged the arteries of a small army, and feeling a little self-conscious in the tracksuit and trainers that she had borrowed from her tutor.

The two of them began to walk towards the exit of the car park, and the trainers squeaked a little on the concrete floor as Jess's feet slipped slightly inside them. Her own boots were tucked safely inside the black kit bag that bounced against her back, and Jess was quietly looking forward to getting back into her uniform.

'If astral projection takes years of practice, does that mean being a ghost takes years of practice, too?' Jess wondered, and Jackson raised his eyebrows.

'Surprisingly perceptive, Jess. Yes, it basically does. New ghosts are like puppies,' he muttered.

'Are they cute?'

'No, they're bloody useless and require a lot of cleaning up after them. But eventually, if they learn, they can either be pretty useful or really bloody scary, depending on how they grow up.'

Jess nodded thoughtfully, thinking about the

booming slam of doors in her own hallway as she'd pelted out into the night.

'So…' Jess began hesitantly, 'can ghosts talk to humans? Or can they only talk to people who are projecting onto the astral plane?'

'Only on the astral plane,' Jackson groaned, as they walked across the concrete. 'Otherwise, I'm sure you'd hear the strains of whatever poor lost souls haunt this car park, telling you to save the interrogation for your suspects.'

The sound of Jess's squeaking trainers faded away as they headed out of the nearly empty car park, into the bright early-morning sun.

As they walked down the pavement towards the police station, Jess stepped aside to allow a group of three men travelling in the opposite direction to pass. Two of them hulked large and brooding in long black coats, whereas the third was slightly smaller, with a long, camel-coloured coat, belted across a well-cut suit. His heavy black eyebrows and receding hairline looked strangely familiar as he nodded to Jess.

'Mornin' officers,' he said politely in a broad Estuary drawl, and continued on his way down the path. After a moment, Jess frowned and turned to PC Jackson, whose customary scowl was now positively thunderous.

'So, now you've met the lovely Charlie Benson,' he snarled. 'You've probably seen his mug shot around in the station. Nasty piece of work, and he likes to remind us that he knows exactly who all the local officers are.'

'Wait – but we just walked right past him,' Jess protested, bewildered.

'Did you see him commit a crime? No. And you probably never will, we never do, and that's the problem,' Jackson snapped. 'The world and its mum knows he's behind half the drugs moving through this town, but we never actually see him do it, and no one wants to talk. That's why he just keeps walking around, being a prick.'

'So, we can't arrest him?' Jess asked, and Jackson snorted.

'In the nicest possible way, Jess, we're not exactly the kind of officers who were likely to arrest him anyway,' he reminded her, and she nodded.

They turned onto the street where the police station squatted, a huge concrete block that stared passively onto the busy main road below. Jess turned to her tutor, hoping to squeeze in just a few last questions before she went back to pretending that she barely knew him.

'Do you do anything else with projection, other than banishing ghosts?' she asked, and Jackson nodded.

'We… well, I guess you could say we keep the peace,' he said, shrugging.

'What do you mean?'

'You know I mentioned new ghosts? Well, if we can get to them quickly, we can have a surprisingly big influence on how they turn out,' he told her, and Jess raised her eyebrows.

'How do you do that?'

'Well, it helps being a police officer.'

'Why?'

'Let me put it this way, Jess, not many people end up seeing a freshly dead body on an average day at work,' Jackson told her dryly.

'Is that… normal?' Jess asked worriedly, as they swung open the doors to the station and stepped inside.

*

A few hours later, Jess found herself standing with one of the first Huntshire civilians who didn't seem actively displeased to see her. This was mostly because he was dead.

Jess had been dreading the moment she saw her first body on the job. Until now, she wasn't sure whether staring into a set of lifeless eyes would be enough to make her turn tail and run straight back into the first safe, boring office job she could find.

Luckily, as she stood in front of the still-hanging corpse of Bill James, suspended from a sturdy balcony over a dusty warehouse, she felt nothing but a twinge of sympathy for the stranger who had taken his own life several hours before. He was still dressed for work in his grubby overalls and steel-capped boots, with the grim addition of the thick hemp rope now wrapped around his heavily bruised neck.

At least he had presumably found peace from

whatever was troubling him, in the sad and final moments when he kicked away the battered metal chair, which now lay forlornly on its side beneath his limp feet.

PC Jackson stood by Jess's side, also looking up at Bill. When he spoke to her, his tone was surprisingly gentle.

'Is this the first time you've seen a body?' he asked quietly, his voice echoing slightly among the tall metal shelves of the warehouse.

Jess nodded her head, wordlessly. For some time, the two of them stood silently in front of Bill's body, listening to the faint sounds of the offices upstairs.

Bill, it seemed, had been the manager of the warehouse they now stood in. When one of his colleagues had arrived to find him dangling from a metal rail, the owner of the company had made the wise decision to head off the rest of the staff at the front door, telling them there had been an accident.

They could now hear him running around upstairs, frantically trying to carry out the jobs of about eight different people, attempting to keep the company moving whilst shielding his workforce from the inevitable tragic news to come. Jess really liked him for that.

'What happens now?' Jess asked eventually, tearing her gaze away from Bill's face. The one thing she couldn't quite get used to was the fact that Bill's eyes were still slightly open, and utterly blank, as he stared away across the warehouse he used to run.

'Well, the inspector's on his way, and will give us

the official verdict. If there was any doubt at all that he was actually dead, we'd take him down… but if it's a definite body, we don't move it until it's all confirmed that there's been nothing, you know, *untoward* going on.'

'Surely in this case, it's obviously a suicide?'

'I mean… yes, logically I would agree. Sometimes it's a formality. But it makes sense to do it, just in case.'

'Sure.'

'Right,' Jackson announced stiffly, 'let's get on with the sudden death paperwork.'

He was holding a wedge of forms, which he carried over to a battered folding table that squatted in the gloom of the warehouse, a short distance away from Bill's body. Jess followed him reluctantly, glancing back over to Bill as she did so.

'It feels weird, filling in forms while he's just… hanging there.'

'Yup. It's all part of the job, I'm afraid,' Jackson muttered, and slid the forms over to Jess as she sat down next to him at the table. 'You should do these, so you get the experience.'

Jess nodded and bent her head over the paperwork, trying to concentrate on the sheet of paper in front of her, and not the silently hanging corpse. She couldn't resist another glance up at Bill James, as an uncomfortable thought formed in her mind.

'Do you think… is there a chance that Bill is… well, do you think he's still 'here'?' Jess asked PC Jackson slowly.

'Do I think he's a ghost?' Jackson mused, looking up at the body. 'Good question. Not everyone does come back, but there's only one way to find out, really.'

Jess turned to look at him, raising her eyebrows in surprise.

'You mean you're going to project?' she muttered, looking around the empty warehouse.

'Well… not now, but later. Though I'd need some help,' he replied quietly, looking questioningly at Jess. She nodded slowly.

'So, you wouldn't be banishing him, you'd be… "keeping the peace"?' she asked him wryly, and he nodded back. 'Okay. I can do that,' she replied, trying to repress the excited grin that was now threatening to break across her face. Jackson tapped the paperwork in front of her meaningfully.

'Forms first. Fun later,' he told her sternly, and Jess couldn't help but notice the smile that her tutor wasn't suppressing either.

5

As they drew up outside the warehouse, now silent and abandoned for the night, Jess felt a strange sense of déjà vu. However, this time, neither she nor PC Jackson were equipped with their vests, kit or radios - and Jess distinctly hoped this wouldn't be to their disadvantage.

She sat awkwardly in the passenger seat of Jackson's car, balancing the small wooden chest as carefully as she could on her lap. In the back of the car, a large black kit bag was currently hiding the dagger and gloves from view. Jess found herself very conscious of the blade's presence in the back seat, although she was quietly glad her tutor hadn't asked her to handle it yet.

The chest, however, she felt she could cope with. Tracing her fingers gingerly along the grain of the dark wood, she found herself wondering what exactly to expect.

'You OK?' Jackson asked, his voice snapping her back to reality - if this somewhat surreal evening could be described as such.

He had neatly parked the Fiesta in the deserted car park at the front of the building and unclipped his seatbelt. Jess nodded, looking down at the wooden box. She opened it gently, revealing the tiny bottles inside and carefully pulling one out.

Jess held it up, the liquid inside glinting softly in the yellow glow of the car's interior lightbulb.

'I can't believe this is all you need to talk to ghosts,' she murmured, gazing at the contents of the bottle, which seemed to swirl and shimmer gently as she held it.

'You also need to know what the fuck you're doing,' Jackson replied, with a warning note in his voice. 'Which is why we don't exactly advertise it.'

'No, sure, absolutely,' Jess said hurriedly, passing him the bottle.

'You sure you remember everything?' he asked cautiously. Jess nodded again.

'You project, I wait for you to come back, and then I ask you for the password…'

'Which is not discussed outside the house,' Jackson interrupted firmly. 'This car isn't protected the way the house is.'

'Yeah, but do you really think there's a ghost listening to us right now?' Jess asked nervously, glancing instinctively into the back seat of the car, and then out into the dark car park.

Now that the industrial estate was mostly closed

for the night, there were great pools of darkness in between the streetlamps. The gloomy scene was broken up only by the occasional sharp beam of security lights, scattered across the hulking metal-sided buildings that lined either side of the street.

Knowing that she shouldn't be able to see spirits didn't stop Jess peering into the yawning shadows, wondering if every rustling piece of litter was being moved by the wind, or something else.

'Maybe. It's an idea you get used to, after a while,' Jackson said, shrugging. Jess shivered.

'How can you possibly be used to the idea that someone might be watching you all the time?' she wondered, but PC Jackson just smiled and gently unscrewed the miniature bottle cap.

A strange odour filled the air, which reminded Jess of the mildewed smell of an old forest, mixed with the heavy scent of sea salt.

They locked eyes for a brief moment as Jackson brought the bottle to his lips. Then he tipped the tiny bottle back, drinking deeply. The moment the liquid hit his throat, his body started to sag, and his eyes fluttered closed.

After a long silence, Jess finally let out the breath she had been instinctively holding. Jackson's body was now limp in the driver's seat, head lolling backwards, and Jess leaned in to look desperately for some sign of breath.

She reached gingerly for one of his wrists and gently raised it, feeling for a pulse. Underneath her questing fingers, the strong pump of his heartbeat could clearly be felt.

Breathing a sigh of relief, Jess carefully laid her tutor's hand down into his lap and sat back in her own seat.

From the silent car, Jess looked out at the empty buildings around her. Despite the bizarre events of the evening, the longer she spent away from her house, the more she couldn't quite believe what she'd seen just a couple of nights ago. Her brain seemed determined to rationalise it away, memory by memory, until she found herself wondering whether she'd really balanced her wine glass correctly, or whether she'd just left a window open somewhere that let in a strong breeze.

Was it possible this was all an elaborate hoax? That didn't make sense either. The sound of the piano as it played in the lonely darkness was still echoing in her mind.

She looked over again at Jackson's apparently unconscious form, his hand still sitting limply in his lap where Jess had dropped it.

'PC Jackson?' she asked quietly, looking for any sign of a reaction. Unable to resist the urge, she reached out one finger, and poked her tutor firmly in the cheek. He still didn't respond. Without quite knowing why, she reached out and grasped her comatose tutor's lower jaw, pulling it up and down like a limp puppet.

'I'm PC Danny Jackson, and I'm grumpy unless you feed me three cups of coffee,' Jess intoned mockingly in a gruff voice, moving Jackson's jaw in time. 'I'll take a load of drugs in a car park and leave Jess on her own in the car, and tell her I was busy talking to ghosts, like that's totally fucking normal.'

With a thrill of horror, Jess heard something click behind her, and whirled around.

Looking towards the rear of the car, she saw that Jackson's lit torch had floated up out of the back seat, and was now hovering by her right shoulder, as though held by some invisible hand.

'PC Jackson? Is that you?' she whispered, looking at the empty spot where she assumed the torch's holder must be. After a slight hesitation, the torch wiggled up and down, as though it was nodding.

'I'm really sorry, about...' Jess began, her voice trailing away as the torch clicked back off and dropped with a thump on to the kit bag.

After a long moment, Jess had the strange but definite feeling she was now alone. She realised with a thrill of horror that her tutor had presumably left the car without the need to use a door.

The quiet sound of PC Jackson's unconscious breathing seemed to grow louder in the car as Jess sat alone, keeping half an eye on the torch now lying innocently back on the kit bag. The warehouse at the other end of the car park continued to brood silently in the dark, and Jess tried to stop herself squinting into every shadow.

After a few minutes of agonised waiting, she reached for the car's radio, flipping it on. It crackled into life and managed to locate an unfortunately familiar station.

'Welcome back to the late show, with me, Ricky White - getting you through the night!' it trilled, and Jess groaned. 'Tonight's topic of conversation - are you alone? If so, why? Are you, in fact, the problem? The texts are going wild tonight, and it looks like we're in for a bleak one. So, why not join the chat now by texting 88838 -'

'Nope,' Jess replied firmly, flipping the radio back off.

Suddenly, a loud bang from the direction of the dark warehouse made Jess jolt upright in her seat.

Whirling around, she peered out through the car window, just as another bang echoed across the car park. It had clearly come from somewhere inside the building.

Instinctively, Jess grabbed the small black torch from the back seat and scrambled out of the car. With one last look at her tutor's unconscious body, she headed across the cracked tarmac surface of the car park, boots and heart thumping heavily as she hurried towards the source of the noise.

As she reached the building's gloomy façade, Jess clicked the torch on, swinging the beam up through a thick plate-glass window.

The harsh light flicked across the warehouse's empty reception, and then through a door that stood ajar, leading to the cavernous space beyond. Jess could just make out some indistinct shapes in the darkness, and what looked like some boxes that had tumbled down on to the floor.

'PC Jackson!' she called loudly through the glass,

but there was no response.

She tried to direct her beam further into the gloom, but the light only flickered weakly through the narrow gap in the door. It was almost impossible to see properly into the warehouse, and as Jess moved her torch, she couldn't be quite sure whether she could only see the movement of her own light, or something else shifting in the deep shadows.

Another, fainter bang echoed inside the space, further away this time. Jess pressed against the window, torch still searching frantically, but she couldn't see any sign of what had caused the sound.

Whatever was going on inside, she wasn't going to be able to help from out here.

For one agonising moment, she hovered in the car park, before turning on her heel and running back towards the car. She wrenched the door open and reached for the wooden box, drawing out another small bottle and cracking the cap.

The same strange, musty smell filled the air as she raised the bottle to her nose for a curious sniff. The strong vapour made her feel light-headed, and her vision swam slightly as she turned for one last glance towards the warehouse. Jess hesitated, trying to squash the grim certainty that this might be the maddest thing she'd ever done.

Jess looked down at the black torch, still gripped in one hand. Despite knowing she should sit and wait for her tutor to return, she couldn't shake the idea that something wasn't going according to plan. Leaving their bodies behind and vulnerable might be a pretty stupid move, but her gut was screaming that protecting her tutor came first. After all, what were their passwords for, if not to act as a fallback for this exact situation?

Jess raised the tiny bottle to her lips, threw her head back, and swallowed the contents. It tasted old, heavy and strange, but somehow sweet. The liquid rolled thickly across her tongue and trickled down her throat.

Then everything went black.

*

When Jess opened her eyes, she felt instinctively that something was wrong.

She was still stood in the empty car park, but the light looked different - everything appeared deeper, darker, and somehow muted. The warm yellow glow from the streetlamps was now a cold blue, and the shadows yawned into deep black pools. The faint sounds of the dual carriageway in the distance were now almost completely muffled.

Jess still seemed to be standing on the tarmac, but just a couple of feet away from where she had been a moment ago. She automatically glanced down at her boots to orient herself and felt her stomach plummet.

Lying sprawled at her feet, Jess saw her own unconscious body crumpled on the dark surface of the car park. Her skin looked strangely cold, thanks to the blue light illuminating her motionless face.

One hand was flung out, inches from the little glass bottle that now rested in a tiny crack, the last drops of its contents shimmering lazily on the ground.

Slowly, Jess crouched down, peering at her own pale, still face. She checked carefully for the slight rise and fall of her chest, before looking back up at the dark warehouse. Taking a deep breath, she stood up again, looming over her own unconscious body. The warehouse somehow seemed bigger in the deep bluish shadow of the astral plane.

Jess began to walk carefully towards the building, trying to keep an eye on her unnervingly still form as it lay slumped by the side of the car. She dimly realized that her footsteps were now entirely silent, and her ears strained in the hush to hear the absent scrunch of her boots on the tarmac.

Looking around the car park, it still seemed to be completely empty, but the way the shadows now stretched around her had Jess's nerves on edge.

As she reached the brooding bulk of the warehouse, she peered into the plate glass window, looking at the patch where her faint reflection should be standing. The only thing she could see shining back at her in the glass was the empty car park, and the pale smudge of her own unconscious face where it lay behind her.

She stepped forwards and hesitantly raised a hand to the dark glass. Reaching out, she brushed her fingers lightly against it, and gasped as they slid through.

For a moment, she just stood there in amazement,

watching her own wrist disappear smokily through the glass and feeling the strange sensation of the window pressing in against her projected skin.

Then she heard a faint, distorted rustle behind her. Jess snatched her hand back, turning to frantically scan the car park.

'Is… is anyone here?' she called, eyes travelling rapidly between every patch of darkness. 'Because if you are… just know that without a password, he's going to know it's not me in there.'

The shadows around her remained silent.

She could acutely feel the lack of her tutor's presence by her side as she stood, agonising, between her own unprotected body and the now quiet warehouse.

Then without warning, she found herself suddenly face-to-face with a pair of wild, sunken eyes.

Bill James loomed in front of her as he appeared through the wall of the warehouse, his dark overalls turning him into a huge, towering shadow as all six-and-a-half feet of his spectral form billowed out into the gloom of the car park.

As he lunged forwards, he collided roughly with Jess, and for a moment she stared straight into the whites of his panicked eyes as he staggered into her. She flung her hands up instinctively, catching Bill by the arms and bringing him to a halt.

For a moment, their wide eyes reflected one another's. Then something resembling her training bubbled up in the back of Jess's brain. She took a deep breath and tried to speak in a calm, reassuring voice.

'Bill James?' she began, but the sound of his own name seemed to make the other spirit snap out of his daze, and he immediately started to wrench himself out of her grip.

'Let me go! Haven't you done enough?' he snarled, and he wrestled his arms free, pushing Jess aside as he began to run across the dark car park.

'Bill, wait!' she called frantically, and launched herself after him, just as another loud bang sounded from inside the warehouse. For a moment, Bill gave a terrified glance back towards the building, as he sprinted away into the night, passing smokily through hedges and fences as he ran.

Jess's boots itched to chase her suspect, but her brain dragged her mentally back towards the sinister sounds coming from the dark warehouse. Like it or not, Bill James was already dead, and as far as Jess was concerned her duty still technically lay with the living.

Tearing her eyes from Bill's shadowy form as it whipped away through the dark industrial buildings, Jess turned back towards the warehouse. Looking once again at the shimmering murk of the plate glass window, she steeled herself and stepped firmly through.

Standing in the dark reception, Jess took a second to let her eyes adjust to the gloom, before peering through the door ahead that led into the main space.

Nothing seemed to be stirring inside.

As she moved forwards, her heavy boots made

no sound against the carpeted floor, and all Jess could hear in the muffled hush was her own nervous breathing. She approached the door before her, which stood slightly ajar, and she instinctively edged around it, not feeling entirely prepared to stride through any more solid surfaces.

As she stepped into the vast, dark space beyond the door, Jess could see a pile of tumbled boxes and what looked like some scattered papers, lying untidily between rows and rows of tall metal racking. The shelves stretched up towards the dark ceiling, stacked neatly with endless boxes, tubes, and packets. For such a full space, it seemed un-settlingly still.

The silence pressed in against her as Jess trod carefully on, moving towards the mess. A shaft of moonlight was spilling into the warehouse from a high window, catching tumbling dust motes as it fell and making it hard for Jess to see past it into the gloom beyond. She continued warily towards it, stepping cautiously around the boxes as she went.

Reaching the shaft of light, she took one step, then another, moving into the dazzling beam and through the other side. As she peered into the darkness ahead, she saw the strange, skeletal shape of an empty forklift truck, and another pile of tumbled boxes.

Squinting into the shadows, Jess heard the faintest sound behind her, so slight it might have been a single breath. She whirled around.

Standing illuminated in the moonlight's dusty

beam was PC Danny Jackson.

With a yelp, she jumped backwards, and for a moment they stood staring at one another, him in the light, and her in the darkness. Then her tutor grabbed her roughly by the arm.

'That was unbelievably stupid,' he growled as he hauled her out of the warehouse, slamming them both through wall after wall as though they were smoke. They may as well have been, as the two figures hurtled forwards, out into the dim blue haze of the car park.

'I'm sorry,' Jess gasped, stumbling along beside him as he strode furiously back towards the Fiesta.

He ignored her, and as they reached it, he half threw her towards the side of the car. Gasping, Jess instinctively threw out her hands, to shield her body from hitting the vehicle.

She slammed heavily into the side of it, and for a moment Jess's spectral brain wrestled frantically with the feeling of solid metal under her palms. As she stood there, stunned, she felt her hands begin to slide smokily inside the car. Her balance faltered, and she whipped them back out of the vehicle, before turning quickly around to look for her tutor.

Bewildered, she realised that he had disappeared, although his body was still slumped in the front seat of the car.

For a long moment, nothing moved - and then PC Jackson's body took a great shuddering gasp and opened its eyes. He clambered quickly out of the vehicle, moving straight over to Jess's unconscious body and gently checking her head for any sign of injury from the tarmac. Jackson then began positioning her limbs carefully, until she was lying perfectly straight on the dark surface of the car park.

He stood back up, staring out into the car's headlight beams, his eyes locked onto a point just a few feet to the left of where Jess still stood frozen.

'You haven't done this before, so you'll find it easier when your body's lying flat,' he told the empty car park, and Jess suddenly understood what he meant.

She hurried over to sit beside her body, trying to work out how best to re-enter its space. As she positioned her spiritual hips next to her own solid ones, she glanced up at Jackson, who was now looking down at her physical form as it lay limp on the tarmac. She was surprised to see that his expression had changed as he looked down at her cold, unconscious face - the fury was gone, replaced by a gentler crease to his brow. Then he sniffed and looked away.

She took a deep breath, closed her eyes, and shuffled her whole body sideways, lying down in the position that she was sure her body currently occupied. She felt a strange sensation, as though sinking into something warm, soft, and unnervingly wet. After a moment, it subsided, and all she could feel beneath her was the car park's cracked surface.

She opened her eyes.

The streetlights were yellow and warm again, and the tarmac of the car park was cold under her back. The temperature seemed to have seeped through her clothing while her body had lain there, and Jess felt herself shiver violently as her limbs suddenly registered the chill.

Her elbows and the back of her head felt bruised, presumably from her sudden, unprotected tumble onto the ground. As she took a great, deep breath, she felt as though she was surfacing from a long dive, greedily sucking the air into her lungs.

Jess felt a hand touch her shoulder and looked around. PC Jackson was crouched next to her, his expression clearly relieved.

'Password?' he asked, his voice surprisingly gentle.

'Nocturnal. The password is nocturnal. I'm really sorry,' she gasped, avoiding her tutor's eye.

'Shit, Jess, don't ever do something like that again,' he muttered, and reached out to offer her his hand. She took it gratefully, and he pulled Jess up onto her trembling feet. 'Easy!' he warned her, as her legs buckled slightly under her own weight. 'You're going to feel a bit weird for a while, just take it slow.'

He reached out and gave her his arms to steady herself on. She gripped them for a moment, trying to find her balance. Her whole body felt strangely heavy, and she was suddenly very conscious of every little joint movement, every flutter of her pulse.

They stood there for a long moment, before Jess pulled awkwardly away.

'So... did you see him?' she asked quietly.

'Bill James? Unfortunately not,' Jackson mused. 'No sign of him anywhere. Now look, Jess, this isn't going to work if you're not going to do what I tell you.' She flushed slightly, as he fixed her with a stern gaze.

'No - I mean Bill was outside,' Jess stammered, 'I saw him, and then he pushed past me -'

'You let him get away?' Jackson snapped, and for a second Jess paled as a sudden flash of anger crossed his face.

'I - I hadn't gone looking for him,' she blustered, 'I was looking for you, I heard a crash inside and I was worried, I didn't want to leave you in there without backup...'

Jess trailed off, gazing up at his furious scowl, before dropping her eyes to her boots. They were back to being reassuringly solid, and comfortingly free of judgement.

'You were worried about me?' Jackson asked, and Jess noticed a distinct change of tone in his voice. She risked a glance up and saw that his expression had softened considerably.

'Yeah... I know I was supposed to be looking after your body, so that wasn't very smart - but I thought if something had happened, you might need, I don't know, a partner in there.'

The beginnings of a smile had found their way back to PC Jackson's face now, and Jess found herself smiling back in relief as he shook his head and sighed.

'Fine. It's done now. He'll be miles away at this point, and when a ghost doesn't want to be found...' he muttered, running a hand distractedly through his messy black hair.

'So, what was the noise in there, exactly?' Jess asked, curious.

'I was fine. Actually, it's a little embarrassing - I knocked some stuff over by accident, and then I tried to clean it up so they didn't start checking CCTV and freaking out... it didn't work out so well.'

'So... you were an accidental poltergeist?' Jess asked, grinning.

'Hey, projecting is harder than you think,' Jackson reprimanded her, but she couldn't help noticing the smile that was still gently curling the edges of his mouth. 'It's not all stealing supplies from your unconscious tutor. Properly moving objects around takes a lot of practice.'

'Could you... teach me?' Jess asked, and her tutor sighed, rubbing his eyes.

'You know how I learned to project?' he asked her, leaning back against the car. Jess shook her head, as she leaned beside him and gazed out at the familiar yellow glow of the streetlights across the road. It was surprising how happy she felt to see them shining the right colour again.

'I stole a bottle from my grandmother's stash too,' he admitted, and Jess raised her eyebrows in surprise. 'But she did agree to teach me properly afterwards, so maybe it's about time I paid it forward.'

'Did she bring you up?' Jess asked, glancing curiously at her tutor.

'Yeah… my parents died when I was young, I don't really remember them to be honest,' he sighed, running a hand absent-mindedly over the slowly growing shadow of a beard on his chin. 'Not sure how they'd feel about all this really, apparently they never knew what she does - well, they knew she was a "psychic", but they just thought she was eccentric and imagining things.'

'I mean, I can see their point. I wasn't convinced until I actually walked through a wall,' Jess said, and Jackson laughed.

'Right then. I've got a warehouse to tidy up, and then we'll head home,' he announced, turning back towards the car.

'Um, PC Jackson?' Jess asked nervously, and he looked at her in surprise.

'I think you know me well enough to call me by my first name, Jess,' he said, smiling.

'Right. Sorry, Danny. In that case, do I know you well enough to say that I need to stop off at my house… because while you've been a great host and lent me some clothes, I don't actually have any clean pants?'

Danny laughed, and Jess looked over at him, realising again just how young her tutor actually was under his rough stubble.

'Alright,' he agreed. 'To be fair, I think it's about time I tried to have a little word with your un-welcome visitor. Although, there's a good chance they've found the knife drawer by now, so we'll need to change before we head over. I've got something special for this kind of job,' he added, his eyes twinkling slightly.

'What about me?' Jess asked anxiously, and Danny grinned.

'Oh, my grandmother has something you can borrow.'

'Wait, you want me to face a poltergeist wearing your grandmother's clothes?' Jess asked, shaking her head in disbelief.

'Wait til you've seen them,' Danny grinned, and Jess frowned as they clambered back into the car. She picked up the little wooden chest as she scrambled inside, dropping it back on to her lap and pulling out another bottle. Danny smiled over at her as she handed it to him, then settled back into his own seat.

In perfect unison, they both reached out and firmly closed the car doors, shutting out the chilly night breeze that now whispered through the empty estate.

6

If any of Jess's neighbours had been looking out of their windows that night, they would have been faced with a curious sight.

A scruffy Ford Fiesta drew into the small parking area at one end of the quiet, residential street where Jess's house stood. Two figures clambered out, dressed head to toe in what could only be described as discount riot gear. Faded black combat trousers and lightweight tops were covered with an assortment of black knee pads, elbow pads, shoulder pads and huge padded vests, with battered second-hand helmets perched on top, visors currently propped open. Each sported a small, round, transparent plastic shield on one forearm.

Boots thumped into the pavement as the two figures strode confidently down the path towards the houses, black outfits blending into the patchy shadows in between the streetlights.

Jess's mouth twitched beneath her slightly wobbly helmet. She had never been much tempted by the idea of riot training before, since legend would have it that the training included a wheelie bin being hefted at your head from the lofty height of a second-floor window.

But there was something rather fun about the intimidating extra layers of gear, going in braced for a potential scrap and a lot of ducking. Jess turned to Danny as they reached the front door, grinning at how out of place he looked in his bulky kit, standing next to a rose bush in a quiet residential street. She looked down at her own surprisingly well-fitting outfit, shaking her head in admiration.

'I really need to meet your grandmother,' she sighed, as she fished her front door key from the pocket of her combat trousers and quietly opened the front door. Both she and Danny reached up and clicked their visors firmly closed.

They turned on torches as they headed into the silent hallway, casting their beams over the firmly shut doorways of the kitchen and lounge. Jess reached out and softly clicked the light switch in the hallway. Nothing happened, so she flicked it back into its original position with a small stab of disappointment. The darkness seemed to press in against them as they entered, pushing the front door gently shut behind them.

From inside her helmet, the sound of their heavy boots was surprisingly quiet as Jess led the way upstairs, moving carefully, listening intently for any hint of a sound. The muted hush and deep shadows reminded her for a moment of the astral plane, and Jess heard her breathing get a little louder inside the confines of the helmet.

The house around them stood resolutely still and seemingly empty. They continued upwards, every creaking floorboard echoing slightly in the hush.

Rounding the corner of the stairs, the hallway also seemed deserted - but Jess noticed that some more of her moving boxes had been pulled open, their contents spilled out carelessly onto the floor. She shivered at the thought of invisible hands rifling through her things, in the lonely darkness of this strange house.

Jess arrived at the bedroom door and reached out a black-gloved hand, slowly pushing it open. The bedroom, similarly, was in a state of disarray.

'Wow, this ghost really turned the place over,' Danny whispered, and Jess blushed in the darkness. The bedroom was, in fact, exactly how she'd left it.

'Just get what you need and let's get going,' he nudged her, reaching for an empty duffel bag that sat on top of a pile of boxes and cases. Danny threw the bag onto the bed and looked around at the puddles of clothes, starting to reach for a shirt on the summit of a pile.

'I'll do that,' Jess muttered, moving towards the nearest leaning tower of belongings. She grabbed a few days' worth of clothes, digging through cases for socks, underwear and pyjamas.

She threw in deodorant, a tiny amount of make-up and a hairbrush, then triumphantly zipped the duffel closed.

When she turned around, she noticed Danny standing by the head of her bed. He was running his finger absent-mindedly through the dust that lay on top of the headboard, then peering at his grimy fingertip. Jess scowled over at him.

'Rude,' she stated bluntly, and Danny looked up at her, mildly surprised.

'Sorry,' he muttered. 'You good?'

Jess nodded, still feeling a little rankled at the small finger-cleaned line on her headboard.

'Excellent. Right. Let's go and get set up somewhere a bit closer to an exit,' he whispered, and Jess felt herself shiver slightly. The house had been almost unnervingly quiet so far, but she wasn't sure that really counted for anything.

They trod carefully together back down the dark stairwell, making their way through Jess's silent hallway, and into the unlit living room. The softly shining PVC of the back door stood in front of them, leading from the lounge straight into the dark garden beyond.

As they stood in the gloom, they swung their torch beams behind them, merging with the pretty pattern of coloured light cast by the stained glass of the front door, which trickled down the hallway and over the threshold of the living room.Standing between the two exits, Jess felt a little glimmer of confidence, as she mentally paced the distance in her mind from door to door.

Danny sighed, pulling a small bottle from the pocket of his riot gear.

'This'll do. I'm only going to take a look around, and then I'm coming right back,' he told Jess quietly, and she nodded grimly back to him.

Danny settled himself on the floor, as Jess stood over him, gripping her torch nervously. As her tutor's eyes fluttered closed and his body relaxed into the carpet, she strained to hear every creak and groan of the almost silent house.

For a long time, there was nothing. Her torch beam flicked and twitched from shadow to shadow, illuminating each patch of darkness. After her encounter with Bill James, Jess was half expecting to see someone emerge suddenly through a wall, even though she knew that this time, she wouldn't be able to see them.

With that unsettling thought churning in the back of her mind, Jess continued to wait.

Then in the darkness, something toppled over quietly in the hallway.

After a moment's confusion, Jess realised that the metallic, rattling thump had been made by the little pot of keys and change that she kept on top of the shoe cabinet. In the quiet, she could hear coins roll softly across the cheap laminate floor of the hall.

'Shit,' she whispered, stepping forwards so that she positioned her body, and her shield, in front of her unconscious tutor. She stole a glance at the back door, which was only a lunge away. The only problem was, she wasn't sure how easy it would be to manoeuvre Danny out at the same time.

Then something hit the wall in the hallway, hard, and the stained-glass pattern that shone on the floor shimmered for a moment as the front door rattled.

Another booming thud echoed from the hallway. A shadow had flown across the doorframe this time. Then another, and another. Whatever was going on, it was getting closer to the living room door. What was being thrown out there?

'Hey!' Jess called into the darkness. 'Leave him alone!'

For a moment, there was only silence and stillness. Jess braced herself, gripping her torch tightly in one hand, and the plastic shield in the other.

'Fuck this,' she muttered, and turned to the windowsill, reaching for the spot where she had left the back-door key tucked carefully behind a plant.

There was nothing there.

'Shit, where the hell is the key?' Jess moaned, and turned back to see Danny still lying silently on the floor. 'Danny? Danny!' she shouted. 'Just - get back, alright? We can come back another day!'

More crushing, empty silence. She walked back to his body, twitching her torch between shadows again, faster this time. Her heart was thumping inside the cheap riot vest, and the black clothing felt uncomfortable and unfamiliar against her skin.

Jess stood her ground, waiting.

Then came an unmistakable rattle and thump, echoing down the dark hallway, clearly coming from the kitchen. Her pulse trilled faster as she recognised what it was.

'Oh shit, Danny, it has found the knife drawer,' she breathed, and once again stepped bodily over her tutor to stand braced in front of him. The door to the living room had been stood half-closed, casting a deep shaft of shadow behind it. But as Jess watched, it suddenly banged wide open.

Glistening in her torch beam, hovering a good four feet off the ground, was a big clump of do-mestic weaponry. Knives, forks, skewers and Jess's bottle opener hung there, glinting, sharp ends all pointed firmly at her, as she stood trembling in her dark lounge.

Jess gulped and raised her riot shield.

*

Some time later, when the crashing, banging, yelling and cursing had finally faded away, a new sound could be heard in the darkness of Jess's house. The thump of a heavy fist pounded against the front door, this time reassuringly loud and human.

'Police!' someone called through the door, fol-lowed by the faint sound of the door handle turning. Heavy boots inched into the hallway, and three dark, uniformed figures began to creep inside.

The figures moved quickly down the hallway, towards the open lounge door. Torch beams clicked on and came to rest on Jess's sofa, upturned and positioned to lie parallel to the doorway. Surrounding the sofa, a gigantic quantity of cutlery lay gleaming in the torchlight.

'What the hell?' asked the same voice, as the beams found Jess, crouched bodily over Danny, who was blinking his way back into consciousness.

As Jess and Danny turned around, they found themselves confronted with a bristling trio of policemen, hands on batons, wielding torch beams squarely into their faces.

Jess slowly raised her visor and looked at the bemused expression of the immaculate A Shift sergeant, and two equally bewildered constables.

'Well. What the ever-loving fuck are you two kinky bastards into then?' grinned the sergeant, and for a moment, Jess would have given anything for another flying bottle opener.

7

'Here they come, hide the fucking cutlery!' Packer crowed the following morning, as Jess and Danny sloped in through the office doors. Jess blushed immediately and scuttled to a desk. Packer scooted her battered office chair over and gave Jess a big wink.

'You know, I've got some knee pads that would look *great* on you if you're heading out this weekend.'

'Leave her alone,' Grant warned, seeing Jess's flushed face turn an even deeper scarlet. 'You know, Jess, you should be grateful you've got the kind of neighbours who do at least call us when things sound messy.' She turned to Danny, and her lips pursed. 'Though I would be fascinated to hear what the fuck you were doing with your tutee and a bunch of knock-off riot gear.'

'It was quite expensive actually,' he sniffed, and

disappeared in search of coffee. Packer, Hunter and Einstein all brayed appreciatively with laughter, but Grant continued to frown, following him into the kitchen.

'I've had nothing but shite from A Shift since they attended,' she complained.

'Serves you right for being in a WhatsApp group with the enemy, Grant,' Einstein called over, before turning back to Jess. 'She used to be part of the twat pack when she first got posted here, if you can believe it,' he told her conspiratorially. 'I think they kicked her out for not being orange enough.'

Jess grinned weakly at him. She began to log in to a computer, and while she waited for it to come online, hurried into the kitchenette. As she arrived, Danny quickly vacated, carrying his steaming mug of black coffee and avoiding her gaze.

'Oh, don't make a fucking round then, Jackson,' Hunter called disapprovingly. 'Just because we're not all invited to your teaspoon throwing parties, doesn't mean we don't like a brew.'

'I'll do it,' Jess offered, sticking her head out of the kitchenette.

'I'm alright,' Hunter muttered, and Jess withdrew, blushing again. She busied herself with the kettle, and while her tea brewed, tried to ignore her colleagues' curious glances by tidying the area.

While searching for kitchen roll in one of the battered cupboards, Jess noticed a piece of paper tucked on to one of the shelves. She pulled it out curiously. The writing on it had been scrawled by a number of different coloured pens, and seemed to be a list of names and time frames.

Turner - 2 weeks

Franklin - 3 weeks

Smithy - 3 days

Sarah-Beth - 1 week

Ali-D - 6 weeks

Darryl - 1 year

Hunter - 1 month

Packer - 2 months

Einstein - 6 months

Next to Darryl's entry, someone had written in a different hand, *'someone's losing his fucking money!!'*. Jess frowned and emerged from the kitchen holding the paper.

'What's this?' she asked Grant, who took it from her and peered at it, then groaned.

'It'll be one of those stupid office sweepstakes, everyone's betting on some nonsense. Go on then, you lot, what's this one about?' she called, waving the paper.

Suddenly, Jess's colleagues all seemed to be terribly busy on their computers, refusing to meet Grant's eye. Danny simply frowned at the paper in confusion.

'Come on,' Grant prompted, 'somebody must know. What's the big deal?'

'Ah, it's nothing,' Packer offered, and Grant walked over to her desk, placing the paper down and pointing meaningfully at it.

'Well that's all of A Shift's names, and most of yours, and you don't want me to know what the fuck it's about. So now I want to know, what the fuck it's about. Anyone going to tell me?'

'We were betting on when Layton was going to leave,' Hunter said bluntly, as Einstein stopped pretending to type and bit his lip.

Jess suddenly felt very hot, and became conscious that Danny was now staring at her. She tried hard to keep her breathing steady and her eyes dry as she looked up at Hunter, who had the decency to look embarrassed.

'It was a dick move against a member of our own shift,' Hunter continued, 'and it won't happen again. Sorry Layton,' she finished, and Jess nodded awkwardly at her.

'You're right it's a dick move,' Grant hissed, and Packer blushed.

'Yeah, sorry, Jess. We weren't trying to be harsh, it's just...' Packer trailed off uncomfortably.

'Right. I don't want to hear any more of this,' Grant snapped, as she scrunched up the paper and threw it into the kitchen bin. 'I'm going to the ladies, and when I come back, I expect all friendship and smiles in this fucking office, and if I catch this nonsense again, I'll make sure it's one of you idiots pissing off in three days. All hunky dory?'

The shift nodded, and Grant seethed her way out

of the office door. The office remained uncomfortably silent for what seemed like an age. Jess slowly made her way back to her desk and opened some windows on the computer at random, aware that her vision was getting a little blurry.

'Jess, mate, we're really sorry,' Einstein offered eventually, leaning around his computer to see her. 'You seem really nice, and honestly, I didn't mean it to be horrible. The job's not for everyone, but that doesn't mean you're not really good at other stuff. I was still a total twat though,' he added hastily.

'At least you gave me six months,' Jess joked weakly.

'You can prove us all wrong, though!' Packer called anxiously. 'And anyway, we're all still here and we're clearly a bunch of dickheads.'

'They are,' Hunter confirmed.

For a moment, Jess felt her colleagues' collective gaze flick to Danny, who was still busying himself with his computer keyboard. He didn't say anything. Jess felt a tight little knot of anxiety twist her stomach.

'Don't worry about it,' she told them all, trying to give them a casual smile. 'If I make it past six weeks then A Shift all lose their money, right?'

'That's the spirit!' Packer cried, her voice overly bright. 'Right then, children, if we wait for Grant to finish taking a dump, we'll all be late for briefing. Off we fuck!'

B Shift all scrambled to their feet and began to leave the room. Einstein held the door gallantly for

Jess as she came through. She glanced back at Danny as she did so, but he wouldn't meet her eye.

*

The police radio that morning held more grim news. On their first call of the day, Jess and Danny found themselves in the bathroom of a weightlifting gym, looking down at the slumped body of Terry Haines, whose bulky form sat awkwardly against a row of sinks.

The bathroom was in need of a little repair but clearly well cared for, every chipped piece of grout and wonky tile scrubbed to perfection. Around the body, however, great sprays of vomit had coated the cabinet beneath the sinks, and the sharp smell of bile mingled in the air with the slowly growing odour of Terry's corpse.

Scattered across the sink unit was a small collection of medicine bottles, all opened, with a few lone pills from each one lying forlornly in the ceramic sinks. Jess leaned gingerly over the body to peer at the labels, which suggested an eclectic range of contents.

Danny grimaced as he also squinted at the empty containers.

'Looks like Terry took quite the cocktail,' he muttered. 'Poor bloke. Judging by how much he threw up, he might even have carried on taking them after he started vomiting.'

Jess looked pityingly at Terry, whose head was

hanging limply down onto his substantial chest. His hair was neatly cut, and the jeans he wore were clearly expensive, teamed with a sky-blue polo-neck that proudly proclaimed him as an employee of Waite's Gym. In fact, he looked little different to the other staff they had encountered on their way into the building, apart from his bulkier, softer figure.

And, of course, being dead.

'Want some air for a second?' Danny asked quietly, and Jess nodded. They headed for the door to the bathroom and opened it, relishing the opportunity to suck in some fresher air from the corridor beyond.

As Jess opened the door, she saw Rod, the gym's manager, sitting awkwardly in the corridor. He scrambled to his feet as he saw them, rapidly wiping his face. Jess gave him a sympathetic smile.

'Is there - is there anything I can do?' he asked, looking a little lost.

'We're just waiting for the inspector and some other team members to arrive. We've got your statement, that's all we need for now,' Danny told him gently. The manager nodded slowly and looked up at Jess, his eyes glinting with tears in the gym corridor's fluorescent lighting.

'He seemed like a really nice guy, you know, and he was working really hard - not just working here, I mean, he had all these goals, he wanted to lose some of the weight and lift more… that's how we met him, he was a member here.'

'I'm really sorry,' Jess offered, shifting a little

uncomfortably in her boots. 'Did you know him quite well, then?'

'Not very well,' Rod admitted, 'he joined the gym a few months ago. He was pretty quiet at first, but we got chatting when I did his induction and he said he needed a fresh start, he'd been through some stuff and wanted to do something positive. Then he mentioned a few weeks later that he'd lost his job, just when I needed a receptionist and an odd-job guy, you know, bit of cleaning, rack all the weights at the end of the night shift, that kind of thing. He jumped at the chance.'

'You said he'd been through some stuff - what kind of thing?' Jess asked, curious.

'I don't know,' Rod said, shrugging. 'Didn't like to ask.'

Jess nodded sympathetically, and Rod sighed.

'Yeah,' he continued, 'I just never thought Terry would - I mean, he was such a motivated guy, you know?' Rod shook his head and his lower lip started to tremble. 'I'm sorry,' he choked, and Jess started forwards automatically, taking his shoulders in her hands.

'It's OK,' she told him, 'you gave him a job and a place to train, it sounds like that meant a lot to him. It's a terrible thing that's happened, but that doesn't mean you need to feel terrible about it.'

Rod looked up and met her gaze, his eyes still full of tears.

'Why don't I make you a nice cup of tea while we wait for the inspector?' Jess offered.

'Actually, I'll make the tea,' Danny interrupted, winking at Jess. She shrugged, not meeting his eye. Danny frowned slightly as he caught her expression, but turned back to Rod.

'Why don't you show me where the kitchen is?' Danny asked him, and Rod nodded, before starting to lead the way down the corridor. 'You handled that well,' Danny said quietly to Jess, giving her one last quizzical glance as he walked away. 'You stay with Terry, I'll be back in a minute.'

Jess nodded and hovered uncertainly outside the bathroom door, unsure of whether duty dictated that she ought to be in the room with the body. She leaned against the cool wall of the corridor, feeling the ridges of the painted bricks underneath her fingers, and enjoyed a brief moment of calm.

She was quietly dreading that evening, when she would have to return to her tutor's house and share an awkward meal before retiring to his threadbare sofa. Every time she looked at him, all she could picture was the resolutely blank expression on his face that morning as he'd tried to pretend that he couldn't hear the discussion in their office.

Was it really so unreasonable to ask for a tutor who would speak up on her behalf? Or was he simply assuming she would soon leave or be kicked out anyway, so it didn't matter?

Her reverie was interrupted by a sudden noise from behind the door. As her head whipped around, Jess could have sworn that she heard a faint clattering sound - coming from a bathroom with no living occupants and no windows. She stiffened, and with one hand on her baton, turned and opened the door.

The room was almost as she'd left it, with Terry's body still perfectly positioned in exactly the same pose. She took a cautious step forwards, before realising that there were now just a few more loose pills lying on the tiled floor. A glance up at the sinks also showed the bottles were in a very slightly different position, as though someone had touched or turned them, trying to get a better look.

Jess gripped the baton handle, looking at the toilet stalls. She was confident they couldn't have missed anyone in here when they first arrived, and even if they had, surely they couldn't have hidden so quickly.

She trod carefully forwards, keeping her eyes on the stall doors, and gently pushed open the first one. Nothing there but an immaculately scrubbed toilet and slightly trailing toilet roll.

The same in the second, the same in the third.

Jess began to approach the fourth and final stall door, closest to Terry's body. She had to step over him slightly to get to the door, telling herself that she was only holding her breath against the smell.

She pushed the door.

'Um, hello?'

Jess jumped and whirled around, half tripping over Terry's clammy corpse.

In the doorway to the bathroom stood a young blonde woman, dressed in the same uniform polo shirt as Terry and Rod, looking nervous. Her badge announced that her name was Faye, and her well-toned arms backed up the job description inscribed underneath of 'Fitness Expert'. She looked shaken.

'Oh God, you scared me half to death!' Jess gasped, and then glanced down apologetically at Terry. She tried to lean nonchalantly against the toilet stall door, which began to swing open, then gave up and rocked nervously in her boots instead, trying desperately to look professional. 'Can I help you?'

'Um, yes,' Faye said awkwardly, 'I was wondering if I could show you something?'

'Right,' Jess said, stepping gingerly back over Terry's corpse. 'What do you need to show me?'

'It's about Terry,' Faye told her, staring down at the body, looking terrified. 'I just checked the CCTV from last night.'

8

'He normally stays right til the end, locks up and stuff, when Rod's not here,' Faye said nervously, as Jess and Danny squeezed in behind her chair in the narrow office, peering down at the computer screen. Faye was clicking through folders, her well-groomed eyebrows furrowed as she hunted around for video files.

The office was strangely dim compared to the bright fluorescent lights of the corridors outside, with heavy blinds across the window and a tasteful anglepoise lamp throwing a beam across the desk in front of them.

Pictures of the Waite's Gym team adorned the walls, and Jess couldn't help glancing up at one that must have been taken quite recently - Terry stood proudly in the front row of the group, surrounded by his toned, well-groomed colleagues.

'Do you often watch the CCTV here, Faye?'

Danny asked, frowning as he leaned over the desk and peered at the folders she was digging through onscreen.

'Um, no, Rod usually does it. But he was a bit upset this morning, you know, and he realised he hadn't done it, and I think he... he wasn't ready to see Terry? But I thought you guys might need it or something, so I volunteered to find it...'

Something about Faye's tone of voice indicated that she was already regretting this particular course of action.

'OK. So, what did you want to show us?' Jess prompted, as Faye finished opening a set of windows and hit play.

The timecode on the screen showed they were now watching a series of feeds from Waite's Gym at 00.28am, and showed it almost entirely empty, apart from the large figure of Terry carefully racking weights in the main gym. He finished tidying the area, and then lumbered off towards the doors to the reception.

Jess instinctively turned to look at the feed from the reception area, but then Faye lifted one perfectly manicured nail and pointed to the racks.

'So, these weights here aren't that heavy, but they're about 10-15kg each. And the racks are pretty strong.'

As she spoke, something twitched in the flickering CCTV image she was pointing to. One of the weights from the centre of the rack suddenly tumbled down, as though it had been yanked out of position.

On the screen, Terry whirled around, presumably reacting to the noise of such a heavy object hitting the hard gym floor.

As they watched, he stood nervously frozen for a moment, before starting to inch carefully across the gym towards the fallen weight. Just as he reached the centre of the floor, it happened.

The weight suddenly swung upwards as though gripped by some invisible hand, then launched itself at one of the mirrors that was mounted on the wall next to the weights area. The glass shattered into jagged fragments that shot towards the polished floor, and Terry launched himself backwards. He ran for the door to the reception.

Jess and Danny leaned in closer, watching the figure onscreen pelting through the gym. As Terry was about to reach the front doors, a plant toppled over in front of them. He jumped backwards and started running for a different door. As he sprinted, he crossed out of the camera's field of view.

He didn't emerge again for a long moment, and the seconds rolled by on the timecode as they watched. Then he calmly walked out again, heading back towards the main gym doors.

His stride was purposeful, and his demeanor looked completely different to the frantic, terrified figure that they had just watched running through the gym. He seemed taller, calmer, and moved efficiently across the reception space before heading directly for the corridor that led to the men's toilets.

In moments, he had crossed the corridor's narrow space and swung open the toilet door. As he disappeared inside, Jess realised there was no feed to show them the interior. The door simply swung shut, leaving a set of still and empty frames as the seconds and minutes ticked on.

Terry did not emerge again.

Danny leaned across and tapped the keyboard, bringing the ticking timecode to a halt.

'OK. Faye, thank you for showing us this. We're going to take this from here, don't you worry. Now look, you've had a hell of a shock, and I think you should ask Rod to let you go home for the day.'

'But –' Faye protested, as Danny helped her gently up from her chair.

'No, really, this is in safe hands,' he insisted, guiding her from the room. As they reached the door, he fished in his pocket for something and turned back to Jess, throwing the small object across the room.

She reached out and caught it, fumbling slightly as she did so, then turned it over in her fingers. It was a small silver memory stick.

'Take the files on that,' he told her sharply, and left the room with Faye. Jess sat down hurriedly and plugged in the stick, reaching for the mouse. Her eyes were drawn back to the closed bathroom door.

With a deep breath, she began to copy the files.

*

'This can't be good,' Danny muttered to Jess some hours later, once they were alone outside the gym. They stood together in the narrow alley that led to the gym's back door, and a stiff breeze ruffled Jess's hair. It carried a hint of the overflowing bins which lined the alley, but Jess was currently grateful to smell anything which cleared her nostrils of Terry's decaying scent.

'Yeah,' Jess agreed, 'if lifting an object is hard, I don't really want to meet whatever was throwing dumbbells around.'

She felt a faint shiver pass through her, despite the sunshine that warmed the alley around them.

'I meant the CCTV isn't good,' Danny sighed, 'and there might be backups of those files. Fuck's sake, I don't even know where those cameras were, I definitely didn't see them while we were in there,' he complained, and Jess frowned at him.

'Yeah… but isn't it a good thing, in the end? Now we know there's something weird going on here, and we can investigate. I know you don't want the general public finding out about ghosts, but honestly, I think people either believe in them anyway, or will just insist the evidence is fake.'

'Hmmm,' Danny mused, fiddling distractedly with his radio. 'I think I might need to contact my grandmother, see if she can come back early, just in case. Things can get a bit complicated after such a clear sighting.'

'So, do you definitely think it's a ghost, then?' Jess asked.

'What else do you think that was, Jess?' Danny snapped. 'Magic?'

'Alright, I only found out they were real two days ago, give me a break,' she snapped back, and Danny peered at her, his eyes narrowing.

'Everything OK?' he asked, and she nodded back stiffly.

They leaned together against the wall of the gym, squinting out into the late afternoon sunlight.

'Danny,' Jess asked eventually, 'are we assuming at this point that Terry killed himself because he saw the ghost?'

'Well... he won't have seen the actual ghost. Unless you're projecting, you can't see them.'

'Yes, I know that,' Jess snapped. 'I'm asking you whether you think it was a suicide or a murder, Danny.' He looked up at her, frowning slightly. Jess took a deep breath and ploughed on.

'Okay. So, we see something that we assume is a ghost, right? Then Terry runs away from it, and then... *something* happens off screen, and it's suddenly like he's not Terry anymore. So, when he killed himself... this might sound crazy, but are we sure it was him doing that?'

Danny turned to study her for a long moment, his arms folded, and a frown darkening his face despite the bright afternoon sun.

'I'm going to be honest, Jess, that does sound a bit crazy,' Danny said firmly, but his tone seemed uncertain. 'I'm afraid in this job, you'll have to get used to the fact that a lot of people simply do want to go out… on their own terms. Maybe because they've interacted with a ghost, maybe something else.'

Jess nodded slowly, shivering slightly as she thought back to the limply hanging body of Bill James, suspended in between the towering shelves of the warehouse.

'Either way,' Danny said, interrupting her rumination, 'we need to get this cleaned up. Then we can forget about it and go back to sorting out your poltergeist problem.'

'Right. And when you say "cleaned up", can I just clarify, what exactly are we talking about this time?' Jess asked quietly.

'Jess, I know you're not very comfortable with the idea of banishing ghosts, but I must admit, I'm a little suspicious myself about how exactly Terry died. And we know either way that this thing is heaving weights around. I think we need it gone, and it's not coming quietly.'

Jess nodded slowly as the gravity of the situation slowly began to sink in. Her mind wandered back to the dagger that presumably still lay in Danny's dining room, its ominously pale tip hidden inside the leather sheath.

They both jumped slightly as their radios suddenly crackled into life.

'VG, Sierra Romeo 2 5, I've got a burglary on an immediate, on Edgemoor Road. Suspect seen on foot heading down Bridge Gardens, grey tracksuit, blue cap, white trainers.'

'Sierra Romeo 2 5, received,' Danny replied, as they ran back to the police car. 'We'll talk more later. Let's get back to chasing suspects still fucking around on this mortal coil, shall we?'

They hurled themselves into the front seats, and Danny punched on the sirens as the car screamed out of the car park, and into the otherwise still afternoon.

9

'Look, I don't like this any more than you do, but I can't wait till you're back,' Danny moaned, pacing around outside his beaten-up Fiesta with his phone clamped grumpily to his ear.

Jess leaned against the car, the cool night air helping to keep her awake after another tiring shift. It had turned into a long night, as they waited for the streets around the gym to be completely quiet.

They had parked up in a quiet residential road not far from Waite's Gym, once again dressed in the base layers of their budget riot gear. The full pads and helmets were tucked safely inside the black kit bag that nestled at Danny's feet, to hide them from prying eyes. Her tutor had suggested they might like to be a little subtler with their entrance this time, since they were planning to physically trespass on the premises.

'Yes, Grandma, I'm being very careful. Yes, I've got a jumper on,' Danny sighed, and Jess tried to suppress a smile. He turned to her and leaned away from the phone. 'Jess, my grandmother would also like to know if you're warm enough.'

'Tell her I'm toasty. Oh, and thanks for all the gear!' Jess called towards the handset.

'She says she's fine and thanks for letting her borrow your things.' Danny rolled his eyes as the phone chattered away. 'We've been over this. Yes, she's a very nice girl. No, I shouldn't have got her all wrapped up in this. Yes, we'll both get a good night's sleep. Love you too, Grandma. Bye.'

He hung up the phone, and sighed.

'She seems sweet,' Jess offered, but Danny just rolled his eyes again and put the phone away.

'I once saw her fight a feral ghost that was a good seven feet tall, but she still acts like the common cold is one of the four horsemen of the apocalypse,' he grumbled, as they locked up the Fiesta and started walking up the road towards the now empty gym.

'Feral ghost?' Jess asked nervously.

'Ah, yes. Your education into the supernatural continues,' Danny said wryly, as they headed up the dark alleyway, and arrived at the gym's back door. He pulled a small key out of his pocket and slipped it into the lock.

'Hang on a second,' Jess interrupted, 'did you steal that while we were here?'

'Yup,' Danny agreed, 'it was pretty obvious we'd need to get in once I'd seen that footage. We'll just delete the CCTV again when we're done.'

'Doing a great job representing the law tonight, aren't we?' Jess said, shaking her head.

'Well, unfortunately there isn't a great deal of law in place for the dead,' Danny replied, suddenly serious. 'So tonight, it's us or nothing.'

He pushed the door, which creaked ominously open to reveal a dark, empty hallway. They edged inside, and Danny pulled the door firmly closed behind them. As it swung shut with a clang, the lights bleeding in from outside disappeared.

Jess's eyes took a moment to adjust to the new darkness, now only illuminated by a soft spill from a door that stood at the other end of the corridor, and the faint glow of the 'Exit' sign which hung over their heads.

'So, where do you want to set up?' Jess asked nervously, as Danny dropped the kit bag on the floor and started pulling out their riot gear.

'First things first, get strapped in,' he said, throwing her a pair of knee pads.

Jess nodded and started to pull her padding on, keeping a wary eye on the dark length of the corridor. She struggled to get her shoulder pads in place, fiddling awkwardly with the straps. As she wrestled with the Velcro, she felt a bigger, rougher hand close over her own.

'I've got it,' Danny said, and gently fastened the straps. For an awkward moment, she realised they were standing close enough together that she could feel his breath tickling her cheek, and caught the scent of something musky underneath the dusty smell of his own battered body armour. Was it after-shave? She couldn't recall her tutor smelling of anything other than stale coffee before.

'Actually, I've got it,' Jess told him awkwardly, stepping away and clumsily adjusting the straps until her padding sat snugly around her. Danny watched her, looking faintly disappointed.

Somewhere in the gym, they heard a loud crash.

Jess jumped and Danny dropped his hand, whipping around to look up the dark corridor.

'So… would you like to quickly fill me in on the feral ghost thing?' Jess whispered as Danny grabbed the bag, and they began quickly walking towards the source of the noise, their boots squeaking gently against the polished tiles on the floor.

'Right. So, spirits don't tend to do too well when outside of a physical body for a long time. Some stay reasonably sane and fine, others… change.'

'How do we tell the difference?' Jess asked, as Danny cautiously pushed the door open at the end of the corridor.

'Well, behaviour mostly. Now, I'm hoping that's not what we're facing tonight,' he told her firmly. 'But if you do see one, you'll notice they become visibly… less human.'

'So not like Bill James, then? I mean, he pretty much looked like when we found him, except - well, less dead,' Jess offered awkwardly.

Danny shrugged, and they began treading softly into the abandoned reception. The empty front desk loomed ahead of them, as the streetlights outside poured in through the windows.

'Human beings have a pretty good perception of how we look on any given day, so when our spirit is outside our body for any reason, undead or otherwise, we generally manifest as we see ourselves. Can lead to some interesting cases where the ghost matches the inner but not the outer perspective. Dementia patients turning up as their childhood selves, that kind of thing.'

Danny spoke very matter-of-factly, but Jess could sense an uncomfortable edge in his voice.

'Is that why feral ghosts look different?'

'That's the theory, yes. As the mind unravels, the spirit looks how it feels, not how it looked when it was alive. It's one way to tell if the spirit still has a grasp on reality.'

'I bet I look pretty feral then,' Jess muttered.

'You looked fine,' Danny shrugged. 'Very strong projection. I think you might even have manifested as a couple of inches taller than you actually are.'

'Really? What does that mean?'

'That you're getting too big for your boots?' Danny retorted, and winked. Jess smiled stiffly in reply.

Just then, another bang sounded from the main gym. Danny held out his hand in caution, and Jess stopped, straining to hear any further noise. After a long moment, Danny nodded and they made their way silently around the reception desk, where he gently set down the kit bag.

Jess padded quietly over towards the main gym doors, peering through the glass and into the dark tangle of machinery beyond. There definitely wasn't any sign of movement inside.

When she turned back, she noticed Danny was absent-mindedly running his finger across the top of the reception desk and inspecting his fingertip for dust.

'Seriously. Do you do that everywhere you go?' Jess snapped, and he looked up.

'Only dusty places,' he grinned, but Jess frowned at him.

'Danny, the cleaner literally died,' she pointed out bluntly, and he blushed, ducking swiftly down behind the desk to unzip the kit bag. He withdrew the large, softly rustling net, which glittered faintly in the moonlight. Jess suddenly smelt a strong whiff of sage.

'Right. You clear on what you need to do?' Danny whispered, as she crouched next to him, holding out her hands for the net. He passed it to her, then began rummaging in the bag again, extracting his torch, the tactical gloves, and finally the dagger.

Jess gazed worriedly at the sheathed weapon, as the net shimmered in her arms. She took a deep breath and looked up at her tutor.

'Danny,' she began slowly, 'if we can catch a ghost, surely we could… I mean, are you absolutely sure we need to kill them?'

'Jess, for God's sake,' her tutor snapped, and for a second she was taken aback by how angry he looked. 'When are you going to start doing what I tell you?'

'I wasn't trying to, look, I just meant -'

'Right, I tell you what,' he continued, rummaging furiously inside the kit bag again. 'Wait here,' he snapped, and without warning, he had suddenly thrown the contents of a small bottle into his mouth. Jess started forwards in alarm, as his body sagged back into the reception desk.

She grabbed his unconscious body and gently lowered it against the polished wood, then stared around furiously at the empty reception.

'What the fuck, Danny?' she hissed, 'could you stop acting like a toddler in a stab vest? Yeah, you heard me,' she added, to his quietly slumbering physical form.

Within moments, she heard a shuddering gasp as Danny woke back up. He fixed her with a hard stare as he did so.

'Password?' Jess snapped, and Danny scowled.

'Spectral. Right then, Jess. Terry's in the gym. Off you go,' he said coldly, and Jess started backwards in surprise.

'Sorry? What, you want me to talk to him?' she asked, bewildered.

'Whatever you want, Jess,' he said, shrugging and holding out a small bottle to her. 'See if Terry's in the mood for a chat. If not, I'll be out here with the net, and you know what to do.'

'Hang on, you need me - to signal you?' Jess stammered. 'I don't know about this,' she continued

109

hesitantly, and as her tutor smiled at her, she felt herself bristle.

'So. Happy to trust my judgement, then?' he asked triumphantly, beginning to withdraw his hand. Something in Jess snapped, and she dropped the shimmering silver net to the floor.

She lunged forwards, seizing the small bottle from him, and opening the top. She breathed in the heavy scent, enjoying the momentary look of panic cross her tutor's face.

'If I get this wrong, I'm not going to buy you cakes,' she snarled, and necked the contents of the bottle. The last thing she felt was her tutor's hands reaching out and gently catching her shoulders, guiding her slumping body towards the floor, as everything went black.

*

This time, she was ready for the disorientating sensation of waking up a few feet from her prone body. The moonlight spilling through into the dark reception had taken on the familiar bluish hue, the shadows stretching longer and deeper across the floor.

Jess looked down at her unconscious body, as her tutor once again positioned her carefully, resting her arms gently by her sides. He then picked up the torch, throwing it casually away from him, so it bounced and tumbled across the polished floor.

'Go on then, you know the signal, pick it up,' he

stated bluntly, settling himself back against the reception desk to watch.

Scowling, Jess bent down to pick up the torch, but found herself drawn instead to the gleaming heap of the net, which now lay puddled on the smartly polished wooden floor.

Jess knew that theoretically, since the net was riddled with sage and silver, she wouldn't be able to pass through it. But she couldn't help being curious about the exact sensation of touching it, and reached out for the silvery folds.

As her hand almost brushed the surface, she felt it flung back with unexpected force, and a strong prickling pain not unlike an electric shock. Wincing, Jess shook out her hand, trying to rid her fingers of the stinging effect. The feeling took a worrying time to subside. No wonder Danny's net was so potent when it came to trapping ghosts.

She flexed her fingers, quickly deciding to try and lift the torch in her left hand instead. She reached down and tried to close her fingers over the black plastic surface. They shimmered through, leaving the torch untouched on the floor.

Jess swore under her breath, aware that she had been almost expecting that to happen. Danny had repeatedly warned her that navigating the other plane wasn't going to be simple, but she had rather hoped moving a torch wouldn't prove this complicated.

Frowning slightly in concentration, Jess bent back over the torch, reaching her fingers out gently, and manoeuvring them gradually closer to it until they were just millimetres away.

Then she took a deep breath and closed her hand again, concentrating on the shape of the torch's stubby barrel. To her mild surprise, this time it felt as she expected - the plastic was cold to the touch, ridged slightly, with a soft rubber button raised at one end. But when she closed her hand fully over it, it felt strangely heavy, and she really had to strain to get it to move at all.

Finally, panting slightly, Jess managed to raise the torch off the floor and carefully stand herself upright. She clicked the tiny rubber button triumphantly with her free hand, and the beam swung into the air as Danny watched. He looked a little irritated, but nodded approvingly.

'See you back here, Jess,' he told the darkness, just next to where her projection stood.

Jess's spectral steps carried her past the reception desk and towards the doors of the main gym. She stretched the fingers of her tingling right hand as she walked, and to her intense relief, felt the strange sensation from the net slowly subsiding.

She arrived in front of the double doors to the gym, whose metallic handles glinted coldly in the blue light. Reaching out, she concentrated hard this time on the shape of the objects before her, and determinedly grasped one of the handles.

As the cold metal pressed against her ghostly palm, Jess grinned to herself. Gripping it firmly, she swung the door slowly open, grimacing with the effort of pulling the strangely heavy weight. Once she had widened the gap enough, she quickly stepped inside, making sure the little torch had travelled through before she let the door swing firmly closed behind her.

Inside, the gym was dark and seemingly empty. The machines stood quiet and still, like a silhouetted forest of metal, plastic and rubber. Peering through the handles and bars, she could see the place where the smashed mirror had hung on the wall before it was carefully removed, leaving a patch of lighter paint behind.

She walked forwards across the gym floor, her heavy boots now making no noise against the hard surface. The torch beam swung slowly around as she trod carefully between machines, shining this way and that through the gleaming metal.

Then something breathed softly behind her. Jess spun around.

The beam of her torch flicked up, and then shook a little in Jess's hand. Her eyes travelled slowly upwards as she took in the sight of the huge, hulking thing which now loomed between her and the exit.

It definitely looked like it had been a person, with four limbs and a big, barrel chest, almost bursting out of the ragged facsimile of a sky-blue, polo-neck shirt. The hair, however, was straggling and matted, and it framed a face that reminded Jess of the kind of horror films she watched between half-closed fingers on rainy nights. Its nails were too long, the fingers were too long, and as the body pulled itself upright, it seemed too tall to be fully human.

The thing staggered a couple of clumsy steps towards Jess, its wild eyes narrowing in the torch beam. Their gazes locked for a moment. Then Jess turned on her heavily booted heel and ran.

She headed straight for the back wall of the gym, hoping to feint and lead the thing aside so that she could bolt frantically for the door.

The feral ghost's twisted feet made no sound against the gym floor, but its breath was getting louder and louder behind her as it closed the gap. Jess had only metres to go until the wall, and the slavering noise of the approaching ghost was so loud now that it was almost overwhelming.

Jess ducked left and slid through the reaching, metal arms of a machine, leaving the ghost to belt wildly past her. She almost smiled as she finished her skidding turn inside the equipment, passing gently through as though it were simply a thick cloud. Then something caught her wrist, and she jolted backwards in surprise.

Her torch clattered to the ground, and Jess realised with a curse that she had just tried to pull a solid object through the machine with her. Her brain raced, and for a moment she was cast back to the dark car park of the warehouse, as her spectral body bounced off the Fiesta's shining side.

The metal bars around her were cold, and they were pressing in against her on all sides. Jess suddenly felt unbearably solid, and unmistakably trapped. She was panicking now, her own breath coming ragged and loud, and it seemed to fill her mind as she struggled to concentrate on walking back out of the machine.

Then something else crept into the edges of her hearing, and she realized with a thrill of horror that the feral ghost had gained precious seconds while she struggled inside her accidental cage. Mere feet behind her, Jess heard a guttural, triumphant growl bubbling from a spectral throat. It had almost caught up with her.

Taking a deep breath, Jess closed her eyes. In the momentary darkness, she forced her thrashing mind to ignore everything that had come before and imagine pure, empty nothingness, just a step away. She dimly realised that she couldn't feel the metal against her arms anymore, and hurriedly stepped forwards.

Opening her eyes, Jess could have cried with relief as she saw that her spirit was now free of the equipment. From the corner of her eye, she saw her torch still lying on the ground and threw herself sideways towards it, knowing that without it, she wouldn't be able to signal Danny with the net.

Her hand passed straight through it, but as she tumbled into the gym floor in frustration, she felt the huge, sinewy body of the feral ghost go soaring over her, and her head whipped up to watch it plummet past. It must have missed her by inches.

Jess tried to keep her now panicking mind in check, knowing that she had only moments before the thing turned itself back around. Now that she could feel the solid floor, she glared over at the torch, reaching out, willing it to be solid. Her hand connected, and she grasped it triumphantly.

As the ghost righted itself and came back towards her, Jess made one final lunge to her left. It grabbed at her, its fingers seeming to grow even longer as the deformed nails stretched towards her skin. She cleared them so tightly that she felt one brush against her cheek.

Jess pounded away across the floor, heading straight for the exit. She hit the main doors with a ferocious bang, flinging them open to let the tiny torch travel through with her. Only moments behind her, she heard another loud bang as the feral ghost hit the doors on the backswing. It had closed the gap with fearsome speed, and she swore she could feel its heavy breath on her back as she ran frantically towards the reception desk.

As she approached the desk, she saw Danny rise suddenly from behind it, billowing his net open. She risked a momentary glance backwards, saw the terrifying form of the ghost belting towards her, and then threw the torch to the floor with a clatter.

For one horrifying moment, the feral ghost opened its terrible, long fingers, and it screamed in triumph as it reached for Jess's fear-frozen face.

Then Danny dropped the net.

With a final, terrible howl, the ghost was driven to the floor as the net wrapped tightly around it. The hulking shape thrashed around inside, although the glittering net barely moved. Despite its huge bulk, the creature just couldn't seem to free itself. Jess saw Danny take a nervous step backwards, looking at the net as it twitched gently.

Jess tried to steady her breathing, as her spectral brain attempted to remind itself that she no longer had any lungs to oxygenate.

Then she looked down at her unconscious body lying a few feet away, and shaking herself from her reverie, strode purposefully forwards.

'What the fuck was that?' she choked a moment later, as she brought her physical form gasping back to consciousness. Danny wheeled around, turning to stare at her. He was still hovering by the net, and Jess was mildly unnerved to see that on this plane, the gleaming folds looked completely empty.

The only thing to indicate that her howling quarry was still inside was the unnatural hump of the net, curving around its unseen occupant. The folds twitched slightly, presumably in time with the thrashing movement of Terry's feral form.

'Password?' Danny asked shortly, as he strode over and crouched down beside her.

'Ethereal,' Jess said distractedly, her breathing still decidedly faster than usual.

'You OK?' Danny asked, peering worriedly at her.

'Am I OK? Yeah, you know what, I'm fine, but why the fuck would you just send me in against that thing?' Jess spluttered, gesturing furiously towards the net. 'Jesus, Danny, what even happens to me if I get… well, what if he'd caught up with me?'

'Did he hurt you?' Danny murmured, looking Jess over, but she pushed him roughly away and stood up, moving over towards the net. She could almost swear she heard the faint edge of a howl, as the silver folds rustled gently in front of her.

She heard footsteps as her tutor arrived behind her, and as she turned, she started backwards in surprise. He had pulled on the tactical gloves, and in one outstretched hand, he held the dagger.

The blade almost glowed in the moonlight, as he strode past her and raised one gloved hand. As Jess started forwards in alarm, he thrust the blade firmly down into the net.

With a soft clatter, the silver-shot net sank into a puddle on the floor, completely empty. She could have sworn that just for a second, the air shifted around her, almost sucked towards the space where the struggling form of Terry's bulk had been. The smell of sage grew stronger.

Without ceremony, Danny sheathed the dagger again and collected up the net. He strode back over towards the reception desk, leaving Jess staring after him.

'What the hell was that about?' she asked eventually, as he tucked the last of the equipment into the kit bag and headed back towards her across the dark floor of the reception.

Jess stood her ground as he reached her. In their physical forms, her tutor was just a little taller than she was, and she had to look up slightly to meet his gaze.

'Danny,' she continued, her voice now as hard as his stare, 'did you make me face that thing, just so I would toe the line about banishing ghosts?'

'Well it worked, didn't it?' he asked gruffly.

'Oh, I'm sorry. I don't recall you asking my opinion, before you went ahead and killed him just now,' Jess snapped. 'That was Terry, in there, right? Our murder *victim*? He didn't do anything wrong besides attacking me, and even then, I'm not sure he actually knew what he was doing.'

'Jess, for God's sake, do you really think he should have been left to run around unchecked?' Danny snarled back. 'You saw him. And just so you know, if he had caught up with you… getting your spirit knocked around is no joke. Your body might not be hurt, but your mind doesn't know that.'

'So, you were happy for that to happen?' Jess cried. 'Just so I would do what you say? Do you have any idea how messed up that is?'

'Jess, no, I'm really sorry,' Danny said, moving forwards suddenly, his face crumpling as he reached up and took her by the shoulders. Jess froze awkwardly in his grip. 'I shouldn't have done that, it was really stupid. But I wouldn't have sent you in there if I didn't think you could handle it,' he continued, looking pleadingly down at her. Jess frowned up at him.

'Danny, you don't seem to think I can handle anything,' she replied shortly, and he returned the frown in surprise. 'You're supposed to help me

119

when I fuck up. But you decided I was a write-off before I'd even started,' she snapped, wrenching herself out of his hands. Danny stared at her.

'Sorry?'

'I'm talking about my job, you know, the one I'm actually supposed to be doing when I'm not running around at night with you. I heard you talking to Grant on my first day,' she continued furiously. 'Then when people were literally betting on when I was going to leave, you said nothing. Surely you think I'm worth better than that.'

'Jess, it's not my job to persuade other people you're a good police officer,' Danny sighed, rolling his eyes.

'No, it's your job to *make* me one!'

Jess realised she was breathing rather harder than she expected as she finished speaking, staring her tutor down. Danny stared back, then sighed.

'Jess, no one held my hand when I started. Do the job, or don't.'

For a long moment, they stood eyeing each other, before Jess finally looked away.

'I want to go home,' she said in a small voice.

'We'll go back to the bungalow after we've got the CCTV files from tonight,' Danny said sternly, and she shook her head.

'No. I mean my house. I want to go *home*.'

'Jess, I'm not dealing with your ghost tonight,' Danny sighed, but Jess shook her head.

'Then don't. If I can handle whatever that was, I can handle whoever is in my house,' Jess told him firmly, and Danny folded his arms, his familiar scowl firmly back in place.

'Well, great. Good for you. And if something happens to you, then I'm left without a partner?' he asked, and Jess sighed.

'It's not like you needed me anyway,' she said, shaking her head. 'Your grandmother will come back, you can carry on doing this together like you always did.'

'I hoped...' Danny began, and then broke off, turning away from her abruptly, and striding back over to pick up the kit bag.

Jess slowly walked back towards the double doors to the shadowy gym. She peered carefully through the panes of glass set into them, into the dark forest of machines. Behind her, she heard the tearing of Velcro strips as Danny began pulling off his riot padding. She took a deep breath and turned back to him.

'We still haven't found out who killed Terry,' she began, but Danny shook his head irritably, unstrapping the last of his pads.

'Like you said, my grandmother's on her way back,' he shrugged. 'I'll ask her to come back and finish this with me.'

Danny pulled the kit bag on to his shoulder, now half-packed with all their equipment and his own padding. He walked over to Jess, who began removing her own. She reached awkwardly to release the straps of her shoulder pads, and once again felt her tutor's large hand close over hers.

Danny was stood close to her, and she looked up at him as she felt his warm breath tickle her cheek. Their eyes locked, and for a second they exchanged a pained stare. Then Jess shook her head slightly, stepping back from her tutor.

'I've got it,' she said quietly, and Danny dropped his hand, nodding slightly.

'Fine,' he muttered, and backed away as Jess finished taking off her padding. He took it wordlessly, tucking it away into the bag.

Once the kit bag was packed tightly with all their things, they took one last look around the reception. There was now no sign of their adventures that evening, and the space stood as dark and quiet as when they arrived.

'Let's go get the CCTV,' Danny suggested stiffly, and Jess followed him as they sloped together across the room, towards the dark hallway beyond. Her boots squeaked slightly against the wooden floor, and Jess once again realised how much she'd missed the tiny sounds of her own movement.

As the hallway door swung shut, Jess took one last glance at the deep shadows of the reception and wondered what exactly they were leaving behind.

10

J ess arrived into her dark hallway in a foul mood.
She flung her bag down and stared at the mess
in front of her.

During the scrappy altercation with her poltergeist the night before, shoes had been scattered
across the hallway floor, along with a generous
assortment of cutlery that hadn't quite made it
through the frame of the living room door.

She froze as her exhausted brain caught up with
the situation, and a cold realisation flooded through
her. In the embarrassment and chaos of the last
twenty-four hours, Jess hadn't even asked Danny
what exactly had happened here.

But despite the dull throb of fear in the back of
her mind, Jess's temper was finally rising high
enough to overcome it.

'Right, is anyone in here?' she called irritably into
the silent space, and after a short pause, pulled off
her boots.

'Seriously,' she continued, 'I am here for a good night's sleep. I'm aware that I still don't know who you are, and the only person who can give me a proper clue is probably not in the mood to pick up a phone right now. But whoever you turn out to be, I can honestly tell you, I am in no mood for any more of your nonsense.

'In fact, let's put all our cards on the table here,' Jess sighed, 'presumably your end game is to get rid of me. Well, if you want me to move out, that's going to take a while. If you're planning to… well, let's be blunt, if you're planning to kill me, do you want to place a bet on whether I come back as a ghost too?'

The hallway stayed dark and silent, the empty doorways leading to the kitchen and living room yawning into blackness.

'Yeah. That's what I thought. I wouldn't want to put up with me for eternity either,' Jess muttered, rubbing her tired eyes. 'Tell you what, if you are actually in here, and we're on the same page, why don't you… I don't know, knock once for "yes"?'

After a beat, something quietly knocked, once, in the darkness. Jess jumped slightly, but took a deep breath and retained her composure.

'Right. Great. In that case, before I go to sleep, could you please show me where you fucked up my wiring? I'll probably have to pay an electrician a small fortune to undo whatever you did, so can you just do me a favour and show me where they need to start?' Jess asked.

A small teaspoon slowly lifted itself off the floor and began to float quietly down the hallway. Jess followed it carefully, treading softly back into the silent living room. As she watched, a cupboard door swung slowly open in one corner.

Moving closer, Jess peered into the cupboard as the spoon dropped, tinkling softly on the laminate floor inside. Positioned directly ahead of her was a fuse box, with the switch firmly flipped off.

'Oh, you have got to be kidding me,' Jess moaned, as the switch was flipped back on in front of her. Lights illuminated the lounge, and the TV flickered onto standby behind her.

'Right. Great. Well, at least I know where the fuse box is,' she sighed, turning away from the cupboard. 'Good night, whoever you are,' she called, flipping the living room light back off, and walking wearily towards her own warm, inviting bed.

*

'Is PC Jackson not here yet?' Jess asked the next morning, as she settled herself behind the tea-stained desk of her usual workstation.

She looked around at her yawning colleagues, as they steeled themselves for another long shift. Jess felt surprisingly well-rested, having woken up and noticed to her quiet satisfaction that some tidying up had been done in the house. It seemed her unwanted visitor was open to a peaceful solution, at least for now.

'Didn't he tell you?' Einstein asked her as he passed, sounding surprised. 'He called in sick this morning.'

Packer snorted. 'In other words, he's decided to be hungover from home today.'

Jess raised her eyebrows.

'Is that normal for him?'

'Used to be,' Packer shrugged.

'Packer,' Grant warned, 'Let's give him the benefit of the doubt, shall we?'

'Surprised you didn't know he was sick,' Hunter chimed in suddenly from across the room. Jess felt the collective eyes of B Shift all flick across to her, in a moment of expectant silence.

'We don't... I mean, we're not that close,' she said awkwardly, and Hunter snorted quietly.

'Anyway,' Einstein said, grinning uncomfortably, 'I'm taking you out today, Jess. See if we can't avoid a few cake fines - we're getting pretty chubby since you started!' His eyes twinkled at her from behind his slightly smeary glasses and Jess blushed, trying to smile back.

As she booted up her computer, Jess surreptitiously checked her phone, but the screen bluntly informed her that she had no new messages. She chewed her lip subconsciously, thinking that PC Jackson had been remarkably symptom-free when he dropped her off at home the night before.

The sound of her radio crackling brought her back into the present, and she shook herself out of her reverie to see Einstein standing over her desk.

FLOUR PL,
SR.

Alpro

'Right then, probie. Let's roll!'

*

Ten minutes later, Einstein brought the police car to a shuddering halt as they glimpsed two figures hurrying down the road ahead of them. Dressed in scruffy tracksuits and work boots that Jess severely doubted had seen much work, the two men sported suspiciously heavy-looking backpacks and an impressive amount of neck tattoos.

'They fit the description, Jess, ready to go?' he called, and she nodded grimly, heart starting to race.

As they rapidly exited the car, the two men ahead of them turned back to look over their shoulders. A moment after registering the police car and the swiftly approaching officers, the suspects glanced at each other, and immediately started diving off down opposite streets.

'I've got this one!' Einstein yelled, tearing after the one to the right. Jess steeled herself and ran left, keeping the tracksuited figure firmly in her sights.

Her boots thumped heavily against the ground, and she could feel her heart beating hard inside her stab vest, the cool air whipping against her face as she ran. For a moment, everything else faded away as she kept her eyes fixed on the suspect's boots pounding the pavement ahead of her, and the backpack which bumped heavily against his back.

Then suddenly, he wheeled around a corner and rapidly disappeared down a side alley, vanishing from view. In a few strides, Jess reached the mouth of the alley and skidded around the corner, hurtling a few steps inside before realising she could no longer see her target. The narrow passage seemed empty except for a few scattered, filthy metal bins dotted along the cracked concrete.

For a moment Jess stood, bemused, heart still thudding hard in her chest. Then she heard the soft shuffle of a footstep and wheeled around.

The first thing she saw was her suspect, who had clearly tucked himself just behind a jutting wall at the mouth of the alley, waiting for her to run past, before stepping out and blocking her exit.

The second thing she saw was the knife.

'I'm gonna fuckin' bury ya,' he snarled, grinning.

Jess gripped the handle of her baton.

'You're coming with me,' she said quietly, but the man just laughed.

'Who's gonna make me?' he asked, shifting his grip on the knife and dropping his backpack, clearly getting ready to lunge. Jess racked her baton and tried to keep her hand steady.

Then something moved out of the corner of her eye, and she stared over his shoulder, brow furrowing. Following her gaze, the suspect also glanced around.

One of the grimy metal bins in the alleyway was now floating a good six feet off the ground, directly behind the suspect's head. He looked back at Jess, and for a moment, their eyes met in amazement.

Then the bin thumped into his head, and he fell

gently forwards into the mud and concrete of the alley floor.

*

'This girl has been cleaning up!' Einstein crowed delightedly, as they stumbled back through the doors of the office several hours later. The tired faces of B Shift looked up to greet them, raising a collective set of bemused eyebrows at their cheery arrival. 'Three collars, and absolutely no shit taken whatsoever!'

'No cakes?' Packer asked, sounding a little disappointed.

'Not a scone,' Einstein confirmed, beaming at Jess. She grinned back.

Jess sat herself down at a desk, getting ready to tackle the next round of paperwork. As she fired up the computer, Einstein's face suddenly appeared around the side of her monitor.

'So, Jess... can I ask you a blunt question?'

'Sure,' she shrugged, noticing that his bespectacled face looked uncharacteristically nervous.

'You and Danny, you're not... well, I mean...' he trailed off, and Jess realised he was blushing. She blushed back sympathetically.

'No, no, nothing going on,' she assured him.

'OK, good. Because the thing is, I wanted to ask you for a drink - and Danny can be a bit scary, you know? Not that Danny would necessarily be the problem, I mean, you might not even want to go...'

Einstein sighed, and pushed his glasses back up his nose. 'Hang on, I've cocked this right up, let me try again.'

His face disappeared as he wheeled his office chair back behind her computer monitor. A moment later, it appeared again.

'Right, Jess. I'd like to ask you a question.'

'Would you like to go for a drink?' she asked him, laughing.

'Oh, I do love a woman who knows what she wants,' he replied, grinning again. 'Pick you up tomorrow night, after we've had time to wash the blood off?'

'It's a date,' Jess agreed, and Einstein's beaming face slid back behind the monitor.

Just then, their radios crackled back into life.

'VG, Sierra Romeo 2 5, I've got a domestic on an immediate at Flat 5, Cornwall House, Cherry Terrace. Neighbour reports two parties fighting next door.'

'Ah,' Einstein sighed, standing back up from his office chair wearily. 'I think you might be about to meet one of our regulars.'

11

Einstein pulled the police car to an abrupt halt, and they piled out of the car into the late evening sunlight. They jogged together down the cracked pavement, where determinedly growing moss mixed with discarded cigarette butts and the occasional abandoned can.

They made their way rapidly to a squat block of flats, looming drab and grey against the darkening sky. Their boots carried them to a slightly battered front door, which squatted ominously beneath a heavy concrete walkway, its once cheery red paint now cracked and peeling.

They stopped in front of the door, and Einstein gestured for Jess to approach it. She couldn't hear anything from the other side, so she raised a hand nervously and tapped gently on the wood. There was no response.

Einstein smiled slightly and stepped forwards beside her, raising his fist and giving the door several hard, authoritative thumps.

'Policeman's knock, Jess - you'll get the hang of it,' he assured her, grinning. A moment later, a figure could be seen through the frosted glass set into the door, making its way slowly towards them.

Locks clicked gently open, and the door swung inwards to reveal a young woman, one eye almost completely obscured by a vivid purple bruise. Her arm was cradled in a stiff blue cast and sling, and she looked absolutely exhausted.

'What do you want?' the woman asked, sounding nervous. As she spoke, Jess noticed another figure move into the hall. In the gloom beyond the doorway, Jess struggled to make out much detail, but would hazard a guess that the new arrival was a man in his mid-thirties. He wasn't especially large, but still much bigger than the slight woman who stood in front of them, still hovering one hand cautiously against the front door.

'We had a call from your neighbours, ma'am, they said they heard a disturbance from your flat. Are you alright?' Jess asked, nodding to the cast and swollen eye, trying to ignore the hard gaze of the man still waiting silently inside.

'I'm fine. Thank you. Sorry about all the noise, officer,' the woman said quietly, as the man took a step forwards. Jess revised her earlier estimate as he moved further into the light, and thought he looked closer to forty. The woman's voice, on the other hand, sounded like she might not even be in her twenties yet.

'Last time I checked, having an argument wasn't a crime,' the man said, and Jess felt Einstein stiffen next to her.

'Actually,' Einstein replied coldly, 'being violent, threatening or abusive is a crime, as you well know, Shane.'

Jess looked up at him in surprise.

'Ginny,' Einstein continued, his voice gentler this time as he turned to the woman in the doorway, 'would you like to step outside and talk to us for a moment?'

'No,' she said slowly, one hand still firmly on the door, 'everything's fine, thank you.'

'Look,' Shane interjected, 'we spoke to your lot last week when they came poking their noses in at the hospital. She's fine, she had an accident, and now we're back home. I know my fuckin' rights.'

'Yeah, yeah, I know,' Einstein snapped. 'But this is a fresh call, so we're attending.'

'And now you've attended. Thanks, officer. Doing a lovely job keepin' our neighbourhood safe and all that,' Shane sneered, moving to the door and putting his own hand on it. Jess couldn't help noticing how big it was compared to Ginny's. 'Bye now,' Shane said, going to push the front door closed.

Einstein's foot shot out and blocked its progress, and Shane scowled as the officer slowly raised his hand, pushing the door firmly back open. Ginny stepped backwards, looking terrified, but Shane just grinned.

'Yeah, fine, alright,' he sighed, holding his wrists out towards Jess, who just stared at him. 'Come on love, we don't have all day, put the fuckin' cuffs on then,' he leered at her.

Blushing, Jess fumbled for her cuffs and clicked them around his wrists.

'I'm arresting you on suspicion of assault,' Jess began cautiously, trying frantically to remember the correct phrasing under Shane's sneering gaze. 'You do not have to say anything. But, it may harm your defence if you do not mention when questioned something which you later rely on in court. Anything you do say may be given in evidence,' she added, glancing up at Einstein.

The other officer gave her a tiny nod and smile, and Jess felt herself smile back slightly as Shane pushed past her, walking out of the front door. Einstein nodded after him.

'Wait with him at the car, Jess, I'll do the statement,' he instructed her, as Ginny stepped back to let Einstein enter the narrow hallway. 'Don't worry, he's not going to be any trouble, are you, Shane?' Einstein added, and Shane grinned nastily back at him.

'Oh no, officer. Wouldn't dream of it,' Shane muttered, and turned to walk away towards the car. Jess gaped after him for a moment, then as Ginny clicked the door closed, she turned to hurry after Shane's retreating back.

Sure enough, Shane turned out to be a surprisingly relaxed prisoner. He waited patiently for Jess to open the car door, ducking neatly inside, where he settled himself into the seat with no fuss. She closed the door firmly behind him, and then stood awkwardly outside the car, glancing nervously back up at the front door of the flat.

Eventually, it swung open and Einstein emerged, heading wearily towards the police car. Jess walked a few paces over to meet him, keeping one eye on the vehicle's unnervingly calm occupant.

'Everything alright?' Einstein asked, and Jess shrugged uncomfortably. She found herself staring curiously through the car window, to where their unusually passive prisoner sat gazing at the ceiling.

'Yeah, he never causes any trouble,' Einstein sighed. 'He's not stupid enough to give us another charge.'

'But we'll get him for beating her, right?' Jess asked, and Einstein shook his head sadly.

'She's given a negative statement, so she doesn't support any further action,' Einstein explained, and as his face collapsed into lines of worry, Jess realised this was the most serious she'd ever seen him.

'Pretty much every officer in the station has met Shane and Ginny at this point,' Einstein continued dully. 'They argue, he hits her, sometimes he breaks something. We've tried to intervene twenty times or more. But she stays here, no matter what we do, and she has all the information under the sun about how we can help her leave. I just don't know what else we can do,' Einstein admitted, shrugging defeatedly.

'If he's done this before, why isn't he locked up?' Jess wondered angrily, gesturing at the closed car door.

'The sad thing is,' Einstein replied, nodding at the car's infuriatingly placid occupant, 'We've never got here in time to catch him in the act. She'll lie through her teeth for him anyway, because if she doesn't, he threatens to burn her mum's house to the ground. And we're pretty sure Shane goes round for a nice little chat with his neighbours afterwards, because the funny thing is we can never seem to get a witness statement from anyone around here, even though they always call it in.'

'But it's our *job* to stop someone like him,' Jess said quietly.

'Yes, Jess, it is, but the real scumbags can be very fucking difficult to stop within the realms of the law.'

Einstein sighed and pushed his glasses back up the bridge of his nose.

'Right then. You can ride in the back with this charmer, I'll drive,' he told her wearily, and Jess frowned.

'So, we're still taking him in, then?'

'Oh, yeah – but he'll be out fairly quickly. We can give her a few hours away from him at least,' Einstein muttered, and Jess nodded gloomily, turning away from him to clamber into the back of the police car.

She relished the chance to slam the door hard as she sat back in the passenger seat, keeping her eyes fixed resolutely on Shane. He smirked back at her as she sat down, and she watched him levelly as the car pulled away into the quiet evening streets.

*

Later that night, Jess quietly opened her front door, stepping into the dark hallway. She flipped the light on and was reassured to see that the house still looked pretty much intact. Dropping her bag wearily onto the hallway floor, she pulled off her boots and headed for the kitchen.

A microwaveable packet of spaghetti bolognese took a battering as Jess enthusiastically punctured it with a fork, picturing Shane's smirking face as she did so.

A few minutes later, Jess was sat alone in her living room clutching her meal, a glass of cheap red wine perched on the coffee table in front of her.

She cast an eye around the room warily.

'Right then, I'm going to warn you, this is one drink I really need,' she told the empty lounge. 'I hope we're still agreed on no throwing, tipping, or otherwise disrupting the house?'

A pencil rose into the air, and gently tapped itself once against the coffee table. Jess grinned. After a moment, out of the corner of her eye, she noticed a small movement. The sofa cushion next to her had depressed slightly, as though something had settled into it. Jess smiled as she twirled the spaghetti onto her fork.

'So,' she told the seemingly empty space above the cushion, 'I actually had an alright day, for once. In fact, I actually had a spirit help me out at work today, would you believe it,' she continued, and the pencil tapped again, once, against the coffee table.

'Hang on a second, you wouldn't know anything about that, would you?' she asked slowly, letting her fork gently rest in her rapidly cooling bowl of bolognese.

The pencil tapped once.

'Huh. Well, in that case… thank you, I guess,' Jess said, and she noticed the sofa depress again slightly, as though her unseen guest had shifted in their seat. 'I mean, I must admit, for a while I thought it was my tutor keeping an eye on me today. Although in hindsight, you were being pretty helpful, so I probably should have realised it wasn't him,' she continued, beginning to eat enthusiastically again.

After a few moments, she realised the pencil was still hovering awkwardly in the air next to her. Jess wasn't really sure what the protocol was, when holding a rather one-sided conversation with a spirit she couldn't see.

'Well,' she told the floating pencil, 'I guess there's not much point telling you about the rest of my day, it seems like you were probably there for most of it.'

The pencil tapped gently again.

'So, I guess you saw the lovely Shane. What an absolute waste of human skin,' she mused, continuing to shovel pasta into her mouth. It might not have been home-cooked, but the rich, salty carbohydrates were definitely what her body craved at that moment. Her stomach growled appreciatively as she ate.

The pencil tapped again against the table, and Jess paused.

'I'm sorry, I know we can't really talk properly,' she mused, in between mouthfuls. 'I mean, I'm assuming you actually want to talk, and you're not just sitting there hoping I'll shut up in a minute,' she grinned, and the pencil tapped reassuringly again on the table.

The bolognese smelled too good to resist for long, and Jess continued to tuck in, before setting the empty bowl down on the table. She picked up her glass of wine and drank deeply, settling back on the sofa. The cushion next to her was still visibly dented, and she couldn't help but glance curiously over to it.

'So. If we're going to share this space for a while, maybe we could actually enjoy it, a little bit?' Jess mused, speaking again to the space above the cushion. 'I have an idea,' she announced, scrambling to her feet.

Some minutes later, she returned in her pyjamas, clutching a bowl of popcorn.

'Right. You get to pick the film. Tap when I say what you're in the mood for. Ready?' she asked, and the pencil hovered eagerly in the air.

'Okay. So. Sci-Fi?' Jess began, but the pencil continued to hover. 'Fantasy? Horror?' There was still no response. 'Honestly, I thought you'd go for that, it's got ghosts in it,' Jess sighed, shaking her head. 'Something romantic?' The pencil tapped eagerly, and Jess rolled her eyes. 'Fine. I did say you could pick.'

She turned on the television and scrolled through a streaming service until she found a relatively palatable film, which fluttered into life with a twinkling trill of music. Jess ate her popcorn grumpily in silence until the protagonist was introduced, lying in bed with perfectly coiffed hair and immaculate make-up.

'Oh, come on, are we really supposed to believe she woke up like that?' Jess moaned, and the pencil tapped rapidly on the table in irritation. 'Really? Are you annoyed with me talking during the film? For all I know you're talking during the whole thing,' Jess grinned.

Then something slapped at her popcorn, sending it flying up into her face.

'Ah, come on, I was only joking,' Jess sputtered, pulling sticky pieces of popcorn out of her hair. 'I'll take it seriously, I promise.'

True to her word, Jess munched her popcorn in silence, as the film played out to its inevitable, sickly conclusion. The night outside grew deeper and darker as she snuggled further into the shabby sofa cushions.

By the time the film had finished, Jess was curled up at one end of the sofa, cuddling her empty popcorn bowl. There was something strangely comforting about the now gentle presence at the other end of her couch, sitting quietly together in the flickering light of the television.

But there was something on Jess's mind that she simply couldn't shake. As the music ended, she reached for the remote and turned the TV off, musing into the silence.

'There's something that's been bothering me,' she said eventually. 'You remember Shane, that guy we arrested today?'

The pencil tapped gently on the coffee table.

'He'll be home by now,' Jess continued quietly. 'And I can't help thinking what he's doing right now, and who he's doing it to.'

She continued to sit for a moment, then took a deep breath and got up.

'I need to pop out for a while,' she said, and noticed that the sofa cushion moved, as though its occupant had stood up too. 'Look, I'm not exactly going to do this in an... official capacity,' she said slowly. 'I think I'd rather you didn't come. But maybe we could talk properly, soon?'

As she watched, the pencil gently rose one last time, and tapped. Jess nodded.

'Right. I'm not... exactly sure when I'll be back. Look after the house for me?' she asked, and the pencil tapped again quietly as she turned, heading upstairs to change back out of her comfortable pyjamas and face the night outside.

12

The wildflowers still smelled heavenly, as Jess warily approached the front door of Danny's bungalow. She was uncomfortably aware of the late hour, but she could see a faint golden light spilling into the hallway from somewhere inside and hoped fervently that her tutor might still be awake.

She raised one hand and knocked cautiously. There was no answer. After a moment, she raised it again, and tried to copy Einstein's technique - three firm, hard raps on the door.

She heard quiet footsteps in the hall, and another light clicked on. The door was unlocked, and it swung open to reveal PC Danny Jackson, who looked characteristically exhausted and grumpy.

'Hi,' Jess said awkwardly, trying to give him her best disarming smile.

'What do you want?' Danny grunted.

'I... was worried about you. Seemed a bit weird

that you didn't come to work today, so I thought I should check you weren't in trouble, or anything,' Jess blustered, trying to sound casual. 'So… are you alright?'

'Well, I was asleep,' Danny told her bluntly.

'Right. Yes. Probably should have come around earlier. Although, actually… I guess I'm really here because I'm having more ghost trouble,' Jess told him, and he frowned at her.

'Really? More of the same, or something different this time?' he asked, leaning against the door frame.

'Oh, you know, things flying around in the night, that kind of stuff,' Jess replied, and Danny raised his eyebrows.

'Are you asking me if you can stay here?' he asked abruptly, and Jess grinned awkwardly back.

'I mean, I know we didn't leave things very well,' she began hesitantly, 'so I probably look like a massive dick by turning up and asking you for a favour, but I would counter that by pointing out that you were kind of a dick in the first place. So… we cancel each other out?' she tried, but Danny just continued to lean against the doorframe, watching her levelly.

'Or… I could just sleep in my car, I suppose?' she continued, and her tutor shrugged unhelpfully in reply. 'OK. Right.'

She took a deep breath and turned back towards the dark street, faced with the sinking realisation that things weren't exactly going according to plan.

Then she heard Danny give an irritated sigh

behind her.

'Fine. Come in. I'll make you a night cap, you can sleep on the sofa,' he groaned, and she grinned, turning back and following him through the low doorway of the bungalow.

Danny headed down the hallway towards the kitchen, his bare feet shuffling slightly against the wooden floor.

'Want a whisky?' he asked, as Jess clumsily pulled off her shoes and padded down the hall towards the lounge.

'Er, yeah, sounds great!' she called, dropping her bag and watching him disappear through the kitchen door. Moments later, she heard the sound of him opening cupboards, and she quickly stole back across the hallway towards the dark dining room.

Jess trod lightly, her socks making no noise against the floor, straining to hear every sound that spilled from the kitchen. She could hear a gentle clink of glassware as she slipped inside the dark doorway, eyes adjusting to the gloom of the dining room.

She didn't want to turn on a light in case it attracted Danny's attention, but luckily a soft golden glow from the streetlights was gently edging in through the thick net curtains. Jess looked around into the deep, warm shadows, her gaze scanning frantically around the cluttered shelves.

Her eyes finally settled on the dark wooden chest, squatting on a shelf, the gloves tucked neatly alongside it. As she hurried over across the soft carpet, she suddenly realised that she could no longer hear the sound of movement from the kitchen next door.

Jess stopped sharply and raised her head, ears straining to hear any signs of motion. She slowly turned back towards the dining room door, half expecting to see Danny stood silhouetted there.

Then the sound of a bottle thudding into the kitchen side came floating through the wall, and Jess let out the breath she had been holding instinctively. As the sound of liquid glugging into glassware trickled into the dining room, she unfroze and hurried quickly to the chest, grappled silently with the clasp, and pulled it open to reveal its gently shimmering contents.

Jess grabbed a handful of the tiny bottles, closed the lid with a gentle thump, then trod softly back towards the hallway. She had only just cleared the threshold when her tutor emerged, clutching two glasses.

She awkwardly held her hands behind her back, hiding the little bottles from his view. He walked towards her, beginning to hold out one glass.

'Oh, I forgot to mention I like it with ice,' Jess babbled, and Danny rolled his eyes.

'Fine,' he sighed, and turned back towards the kitchen. She heard him set the glass down with an exasperated thump, and hurried into the lounge, where she stuffed the bottles quickly into her bag.

Danny came into the room a moment later, holding the whisky.

'Just how madame likes it,' he told her sarcastically as she took the tumbler, the ice gently rattling against the glass.

'Thanks, Danny,' she mumbled, and awkwardly raised the tumbler to him before taking a sip.

'You're welcome,' he replied, his voice surprisingly sincere. 'Well... sleep well, I guess,' he added, raising his own glass before turning to leave the room.

'Danny,' Jess called after him, and he stopped with a sigh, looking back over his shoulder at her. 'I realised I never asked you... what exactly did you see in my house?'

Danny turned fully back around to face her, eyebrows furrowing.

'What do you mean?'

'I mean, who did you see? Or what were they like, anyway?' Jess asked curiously, and Danny nodded slowly.

'Right. Former owner or occupier, I assume - nothing feral,' he assured her quickly. 'I mean, it's hard for me to identify them without a picture or anything so... I don't know what to say, really,' he trailed off, and Jess nodded slowly back.

'That's fair. I mean, I suppose I guessed that they weren't... out of interest, anything you can tell me about what they looked like?' she asked, and Danny sighed.

'Erm, they were female, young – a bit hard to guess their exact age... they were all over the place so I couldn't get much of a read. I was thinking we

146

could try to find a list of former occupants from somewhere, I'm sure I could point them out easily,' he offered, and Jess smiled slightly.

'Yeah. I'd appreciate it.'

'Yeah? Let's do that, then. Sorry, Jess…' he began, but she shook her head.

'It's alright. I guess I should let you get to bed,' Jess suggested politely, and Danny nodded, sipping his whisky as he headed back down the hallway towards his own bedroom. Jess closed the door gently behind him, feeling her body finally relaxing as the sound of Danny's feet faded away.

As Jess pulled on her comfy pyjamas and got the sofa ready once again as a makeshift bed, she found herself peering curiously at the lounge around her.

She knew that theoretically, it wouldn't be particularly easy to leave the building as a spirit. But presumably she could manage it, as long as she left herself a hole in the defences just big enough to pass through - assuming nothing else found it, and got in.

Jess trod softly over to one of the sash windows, pulling the heavy net curtain slightly to one side. A tangled bush outside the window largely obscured it from view of the street, and a heavy cabinet beside it could easily block it from the vision of anyone looking through the living room door.

It was perfect.

She quickly pulled the window up, leaving a gap just a couple of feet wide, and tucked the curtain aside to leave it clear. Then she moved back over to the sofa, snuggling herself down into a sleeping position.

With her face firmly obscured from view under an old blanket, she took out one of the bottles she had secreted earlier and uncorked it. The smell was even stronger inside her tiny blanketed space, but Jess still drank the contents greedily, and moments later she stood looking down at her peacefully slumbering form.

The lounge seemed a lot more sinister on the astral plane, all the warm reddish hues replaced with colder blue ones. But Jess didn't want to linger long, and found herself hurrying over towards the window.

Then she hesitated, looking down at her astral form. She almost hadn't realised that her pyjamas were gone, replaced with her police uniform, her boots shining softly in the blue-hued moonlight. It appeared that Jess's subconscious had decided she was heading out in an official capacity after all.

Aware that precious minutes were ticking by, Jess shook her head and carried on towards the window. She wasn't sure how long she might have before Danny potentially discovered her secret exit from the bungalow.

As she ducked through the narrow space, Jess felt the aura of sage and silver crackle against her back, like a sharp electric shock.

She grimaced as she pushed through the window, and as she brushed the sill, felt a sudden spasm ricochet sharply through her body, sending her staggering out into the garden. Finally, free of the rippling current, Jess straightened up. Her limbs still burned unpleasantly, but she was grateful for the cool night air which brushed softly against them, massaging her body gently until the sensation slowly subsided.

With one last glance back at her sleeping form, Jess steeled herself and headed out across the dark garden.

*

As Jess approached the now familiar red front door, she could hear the faint sounds of shouting from inside. She broke into a run as she drew closer, and as she hit the peeling wood, she passed straight through it like smoke.

Inside, the hallway lights were dull, but the sounds were sharp and clear. Jess moved silently over the worn carpet, past a towering pile of unopened envelopes that threatened to topple from a shabby end table onto the row of battered trainers that untidily lined the nicotine-stained walls.

She headed straight for an open door at the end of the hall, where she could hear Shane snarling insults, each one punctuated with an ominously wet thud. Ginny was crying harder than Jess had ever heard someone sob, and Jess began to sprint down the narrow hall just as a sickening crack echoed from the open door.

Ginny began to keen softly, and Jess thought her

heart was going to break as she rounded the corner and burst silently into the room. Neither of the figures inside turned to see her as Jess froze in the doorway, taking in the scene.

Ginny was slumped against the chipped paint of the kitchen wall, the arm that wasn't already in a cast now lying at an unnatural angle across her lap. Blood oozed down her face in a river that began from her nose, meeting a further stream from a split lip that was already swelling one side of her face. It dripped silently down onto her shirt, but Ginny didn't seem to either notice or care.

Her eyes looked glazed and exhausted, and she gazed blankly at the opposite wall as she let out another quiet moan. Jess whirled in fury to look at Shane, who had stormed over to the sink to wash his hands. The water ran pinkish red into the basin, and as he finished, he grabbed a tea towel to dry off, before throwing it onto the floor in front of Ginny. She made no move to pick it up.

Shane began to walk out of the room, heading straight for Jess. As he approached, she realised that she had been half expecting the sound of sirens to scream in from outside. Clearly, if the police were coming, they had missed it again. So had Jess.

But Jess wasn't arresting him this time.

As Shane was about to cross the threshold, Jess thrust out a spectral hand, which thumped firmly into his chest. She felt it connect solidly, and a cold smile twitched at the corner of her mouth as Shane started back in surprise.

She reached up and slapped him, hard, across the face. He staggered back in astonishment, towards the sink where the swirl of reddened water still dripped lazily down the drain.

From the corner of her eye, Jess saw Ginny look around slightly, eyes back in focus, watching Shane as he whirled around to look for his invisible attacker. Ginny let out a tiny gasp, and Jess realised it was laughter, a hysterical bubble building inside Ginny's chest and making her slight body shake. Unfortunately, Shane realised at the same moment, and began to lunge towards Ginny.

Jess swung down and grabbed a kitchen chair, which she heaved firmly into Shane's furious face, bringing him crashing to the floor. One of his eyes was closed, the lid grazed and twitching, where the leg of the chair had caught him sharply in the socket. He lay for a moment, dazed, and Jess seized a chance to rush past him and scoop her spectral arms around Ginny.

The woman howled as Jess pressed against her broken arm.

'I'm sorry, I'm sorry, just get up, please,' Jess wailed, as Ginny panicked and struggled inside arms that she couldn't see. Jess managed to get her planted shakily on her feet and began to pull her in staggering steps towards the kitchen doorway.

Turning, Jess realised in horror that Shane was now also upright, and with a bellow he began to charge at Ginny.

As Jess let go of her, the young woman's hands

managed to catch a chair and keep herself up. Ginny's eyes seemed to follow Jess for a moment as she felt the presence leave her side, and then locked into the gaze of her furious partner. This time, Ginny didn't look away from Shane's face as Jess slammed bodily into him.

He flew across the kitchen, hitting the opposite wall and slumping down it, fear stamped hard across his face. Arms awkwardly sprawled at his side, tears now streaming down his cheeks, Shane looked remarkably like Ginny for a moment as he hunched, pleading, against the kitchen wall. His partner watched impassively as he cried, using her left arm in its plaster cast to keep her balance against the chair, as her right arm dangled uselessly at her side. One of Ginny's eyes was starting to swell as she stared at Shane, but her gaze stayed sharp as she watched.

In front of her, unseen, Jess loomed over Shane as he huddled against the wall. Jess took deep, shuddering breaths, and for a moment her face seemed to stretch, her fingers seemed to elongate, the nails seemed to grow.

Staring down at her prey, Jess howled, seized one of Shane's outstretched arms, then raised a spectral boot and stamped down hard.

With another sickening crack and the grisly snick of tearing tendons, the elbow inverted and shattered under her boot.

Shane howled too.

Jess lunged for the throat, her long fingers closing

firm around Shane's windpipe. His howl guttered into a terrible choking sound as he fought for breath, the hand of his unbroken arm reaching up to grab wildly at Jess's hands and arms, looking terrified as his twitching, struggling fingers found Jess's unseen spectral form.

Her eyes blazed wild as she stared down into his terrified face, Shane's own gaze darting frantically around, trying to make sense of his attacker. Finally, he grasped hard on her wrist, and pulled one of her hands back just long enough to choke out a single word.

'Please,' he begged, and the sound shook Jess out of her fury. Her fingers uncurled, and Shane's breath came back in shuddering gasps. Jess took a few horrified steps backwards as Shane began to make a terrible moaning sound, and she turned to see Ginny begin to stagger out of the kitchen and down the hallway, not looking back as she reached the front door and collapsed out into the night.

There were still no sirens as Jess stood over Shane's sobbing body, but she couldn't help feeling a strong urge to run.

So she did.

She hurtled out past Ginny, who was now wandering shakily down the concrete walkway. Jess paused to hammer, hard, on every neighbour's door as she passed. She saw lights click on inside, and faces come to the window. One elderly woman pulled her front door open as she saw Ginny stagger past, and came out in her nightgown, her steps as

153

shaky as Ginny's own. She scooped the younger woman into a gentle one-armed hug as Ginny halted, and they walked quietly inside together.

'Shhh, it's alright Ginny, I know, love.'

Jess watched as the two women reached the golden glow of the doorway together, and the elderly neighbour ushered Ginny inside.

'Now, we'd better get you to the hospital to look at that arm,' her neighbour told her, going to close the door.

'It's alright,' Ginny said in a slightly dazed voice, her arm still dangling at a strange angle at her side. 'I've got some kind of guardian angel,' she grinned, staring through the wall in the direction of her own flat, where the faint sound of Shane crying could still be heard echoing through their open front door.

'Oh, I don't know about angels, love, but I'm going to make you some tea while we wait for the ambulance,' her neighbour told her kindly, as she closed the door with a soft click.

Jess stood in the dark street, still staring at the open doorway to Shane and Ginny's flat. As Shane's sobs finally quietened down, Jess realised she was also crying. She brushed the tears away furiously as she turned and began to jog back into the night.

13

'I can't believe that sick fuck is actually dead. I never thought I'd be so happy to see death paperwork,' Packer stated bluntly, as Jess swung the office door open the following morning.

Her colleagues were already setting up at their desks, and Grant plonked a cup of tea down in front of Packer, looking disapproving.

'You shouldn't say things like that,' Grant scolded. 'A person still died.'

'Yeah, but we all know we'd have been attending for Ginny sooner or later,' Packer retorted, and Jess froze.

'What happened?' she asked shakily, and B Shift looked up at her as she stood nervously in the doorway.

'Oh, you remember everyone's favourite, Shane Wilson?' Einstein asked her, and Jess nodded. 'Looks like he killed himself last night – threw himself off the roof of Priory House. Ginny's in for questioning,' he sighed.

Jess's face fell as a knot of guilt twisted her stomach, and Einstein peered at her curiously.

'You OK, Jess?'

'Yeah, just didn't expect this many deaths during my first week on the job!' she joked awkwardly, and headed swiftly for a desk. As she passed the kitchenette, she nearly bumped into Danny, who had emerged suddenly holding a cup of coffee.

'Morning, Jess,' he offered, and she nodded briefly to him before hurrying past and getting her things settled, not wanting to meet anyone's eye.

'Seriously though, these suicides are getting out of hand,' Hunter muttered. 'It's messed up. At least the scumbags are scumbags, but... I don't know. This other kid,' she continued, gesturing to her screen, 'was twenty-four. Twenty-fucking-four. She had a good job, she was young, healthy, apparently "happy", whatever that even means.'

'It's not like you to let this stuff get to you,' Grant said gently, perching herself on the edge of Hunter's desk. 'You know how it is, sometimes they just come out of nowhere. We don't know what was going on in that girl's life.'

'Well we know some of it, you spoke to her two days ago,' Hunter said bluntly, looking at Jess.

'Sorry?' Jess asked, confused.

'Faye Parker. I'm just filing her death paperwork. Apparently you spoke to her two days ago, witness statement about Terry Haines. Anyway. Her mum found her in the bath. I just... I don't know.'

156

Hunter stood up suddenly, taking a deep breath. B Shift watched nervously as she pushed her short dark hair out of her eyes, and wandered over to Jess's desk, where she stopped, arms folded across her narrow chest.

'How old are you?' she asked Jess, who raised her eyebrows in surprise, her mind still reeling from the fact that both Shane and Faye were dead.

'Twenty-four,' she replied quietly.

'Right, if anything is ever bothering you, then you talk to us, alright?' Hunter barked, and Jess nodded, bewildered. 'Good. Well, talk to Grant, she's better at that. Come on you lot, we need to go to briefing,' Hunter announced, and strode towards the office door, with the rest of B Shift slowly assembling in her wake.

*

After the morning's briefing, it was straight out into their cars, where Jess and Danny drove in uncomfortable silence. They pulled up eventually into a quiet lay-by, and Danny turned to peer at her.

'Something bothering you, Jess?' he asked, and she snapped out of her reverie.

'Um, Danny, what if I told you I'd done something pretty bad?' she asked eventually, and he raised his eyebrows in surprise.

'OK. Define pretty bad?'

'I stole some more projection fluid,' she admitted, and he sighed, nodding.

'I thought you might - it can get addictive very quickly. Jess, it's really not the worst thing in the world, although you'd be much safer doing this with me, not sneaking around behind my back,' he told her sternly, and she nodded gratefully, a little surprised at his mild response. She sniffed slightly, and Danny shook his head, smiling at her.

'Come on Jess, you took something you shouldn't and then you admitted it. It's not like you killed anyone,' he told her, and without warning, Jess found herself bursting into tears.

'Hey, come on now,' Danny told her gently. 'It's alright.'

'It's not alright, Danny, you don't understand,' Jess wailed. 'I went to Shane Wilson's last night, and I - I - I thought I was helping,' she sobbed. 'I just wanted to shake him up a bit, I just wanted him to finally confess what he'd been doing to Ginny,' Jess continued miserably, as Danny watched her levelly. 'And now he's dead! I just wanted to help!'

'Jess, have you considered that you did help?' he asked, and Jess shook her head.

'Danny, there's something weird going on here,' she continued, her voice becoming steadier as she calmed herself. 'Do you really think it's just that people can't cope, when they experience spirits? I mean, Terry, Shane, and now Faye, I just - I can't help thinking this isn't normal.'

She turned to him, her eyes wide and pleading. Her tutor seemed surprisingly calm.

'Define "normal", Jess. Some people just aren't

"normal". And besides, if criminals like Shane Wilson start getting the idea that they should punish themselves once they're beyond redemption, I don't happen to think that's a bad thing.'

The coldness in his voice took Jess aback, and she stared at him for a moment, before both of their radios suddenly crackled into life.

An alarm wailed, and Jess's blood ran cold as she recognised the signal that an officer's panic button had been pushed. Then a sharp burst of shouting sounded down the channel, followed by a short, sinister crack.

As the broadcast died, Jess realised that her nervous breathing was now growing louder inside the car. Their radios exploded into chatter again.

'All units, Sergeant Davies is mapping to out-buildings on Derry Farm,' came a frantic voice from the control room.

'Jesus,' Jess gasped. 'What the hell managed to bring down Sergeant Davies?'

'Sierra Romeo 2 5, we're just around the corner and on our way,' Danny barked into his radio, bringing the engine roaring to life, before turning to Jess. 'Looks like we might be the first to find out.'

*

The outbuilding in question turned out to be a substantial barn, squatting ominously at the end of a field of softly rustling grass. The farm seemed quiet, and there was no sign of anyone else as they drew the police car to a halt, peering through the windscreen.

'Control, this is Sierra Romeo 2 5, we're in attendance at Derry Farm and about to approach the building,' Danny told the radio.

'Negative, Sierra Romeo 2 5, do not approach. Derry Farm has intelligence for firearms and serious organised crime. This is going to be a firearms deployment,' Control replied, and Jess sighed in frustration.

'Danny, that was a distress call from the Sergeant, there's no one else even here!' she cried. 'We need to go inside!'

'Jess, just because you had one good day on the job doesn't mean you're ready to handle whatever the hell is going on in there,' Danny snapped, and Jess bridled. While she knew he was right, she couldn't help resenting his judgement of a day he hadn't even been present for.

But something else had been there that day.

Jess reached gently to her patrol belt and felt the small bottle of projection fluid she had tucked there from her quietly stolen stash. She took a deep breath and looked up at Danny.

'Danny, you're going to need to trust me,' she said firmly, as she began to climb out of the car.

'What the hell, Jess, where are you going?' he called, as Jess began to run towards the tree line on the edge of the field.

'Cover for me, tell the others I'm in position watching the building or something. I know what the Sergeant needs!' she shouted over her shoulder, before disappearing into the trees.

Jess made her way cautiously through the thickets of branches, edging closer to the structure. As she moved carefully along the tree line, she peered through tangled branches at the huge doors of the barn, which had been pulled firmly shut. Nothing stirred them.

Small, smeared windows dotted the walls, and Jess watched each of them carefully for any sign of movement as she trod closer and closer to the rear of the building. As she advanced, she realised the windows had actually been covered from the inside, barricaded over with wood, cardboard and other detritus, to prevent outsiders from seeing in.

Her gaze frantically scanned every tiny gap in the blocked-up windows, wondering whether they were accidents or spy holes for the occupants of the barn.

Her foot came down hard on a rotting branch and it collapsed under her with a sickening crunch, sending Jess toppling into the outstretched branches of a tree beside her. The sound of cracking wood sent a previously unseen magpie rocketing towards the sky with a cry of alarm, its shadow racing across her panicked face as it shot away across the field.

Jess waited for an agonisingly long moment, eyes darting between the windows, watching for some sign of disturbance within.

Nothing seemed to move, so she gently extracted herself from the branches and continued to edge carefully past the structure, praying silently that no one had noticed her presence in the dappled sunlight amongst the trees.

Eventually, she drew level with the rear of the barn, and saw to her relief that there were no windows on the vast, looming wall. There were still a hundred feet or so between Jess and the building, so she dropped low and made a final dash across the whispering grass.

Huge plastic storage butts lined the weather-beaten wall, offering a selection of narrow, shadowy crawlspaces in between. Jess launched herself silently into a small gap, thrusting through old cobwebs and scrabbling against the dusty ground as she wedged her body carefully into the narrow space.

A large spider, disturbed from its hiding spot, ran across her arm as Jess huddled further into the shadows. She didn't even notice it as she tucked her legs tightly against the butts, so not even a boot could be seen from outside.

Then she pulled the fluid from her belt, uncorked it, and drank deeply.

14

Inside the barn, fluorescent strip lights hung cold over the scene below. The space was ringed with a looming tangle of farm equipment, machines, and parts that towered all the way up to the lighting grid, casting strange shadows across the dusty floor.

The ceiling disappeared into the darkness above the suspended rows of lights, and a metal mezzanine level ran around three of the walls, lined with more heaps of parts and equipment. On the barn floor, stacks of boxes were piled high, creating rough corridors in the vast room, which opened out into a clearing in the very centre.

The only movement in the quiet space was here, where men stood in clusters around an unconscious figure on the floor, lying sprawled in his police uniform. Even prone, Sergeant Davies was an impressive sight, almost twice the size of the men who stood near him, some of whom sported a range of nasty injuries.

The Sergeant's baton was clasped in one of their hands, and the blood pooling by Davies' face suggested that he might have felt the force of his own weapon after he lost it.

Near the cluster of figures, two huge crates stood open, revealing a tightly packed cargo of assorted firearms, and a separate shipment of ammunition. Next to these stood another dozen people, clearly grateful that their guarding position put some distance between themselves and Charlie Benson.

The smartly dressed man was leaning against a steel support column in the centre of the barn, knuckles white as he gripped it, face contorted in fury.

'I shouldn't have to fuckin' tell you idiots, that I don't need to be found here with a dead police officer, or a beaten police officer, or fuckin' found here at all!' he snarled, and the men around him backed away surreptitiously.

'So, what we supposed to do now?' grunted the man holding Davies' baton, wiping blood from his own face. His nose looked oddly bent at the bridge and was swelling gently into a purpling mass that was almost certainly broken.

'Well, fuckin' ideally, I want the goddamn van that should have been here five fuckin' minutes ago, so we can stick all this crap, and him, in the back and fuck off,' Charlie snapped. 'I don't even understand how this happened. What kind of dickhead gets stopped for careless driving on their way to a fuckin' pickup like this? I smell a setup, and I think this prick knows about it, so we're not touching another hair on his massive head until I know what he fuckin' knows. Get a van here, and get him in it,' he sighed, and stomped towards the other end of the barn.

One of the men pulled a phone from his pocket and started to dial. The others began to relax at the sight of Charlie's retreating back.

Suddenly, all the lights went out.

Inside the huge looming bulk of the barn, the barricaded windows meant almost total darkness, except for a few tiny shafts of light spilling between pieces of newspaper and wood.

'What the fuck?' Charlie had time to ask, before the first crash sounded.

A large piece of metal debris collided furiously with a tractor that lurked in one corner of the barn. Dust billowed up as it smashed into the ground, and the swirling motes whirled past the fuse box that was fixed to the back wall, its door hanging ominously open.

'Get some bullets in those fuckin' guns!' Charlie roared, as another crash came, this time in the heart of one of the towering piles of boxes. It sounded like something had been rammed into the stack with force.

The cluster of men around Sergeant Davies began to scatter, some towards the crates of weapons, some clutching what they already had, all treading cautiously out into the dark.

Charlie's head whipped around, eyes narrowing

as he spotted a tiny movement in the shadows.

Something was rising up off the floor, quietly, in the deep darkness amongst the boxes. For a second, Charlie thought it looked like a small plastic torch, but that didn't make sense, as nothing seemed to be holding it. Then the beam clicked on and dazzled him.

He flung his hand in front of his face, and as he did so, the beam suddenly swung around. Something crashed through a stack of boxes, carrying the bright shaft of light across the barn.

'Follow that fuckin' light!' Charlie howled, and figures began to scramble in the dark as the light led them away, their feet thundering up the clanking metal steps and on to the mezzanine.

For a moment, the beam hesitated, flickering down over the edge of the balcony and on to the floor below, where Sergeant Davies now lay alone.

Bodies began to close in on both sides of the mezzanine. As they converged around the light, the torch beam clicked off. Dozens of feet skidded to a halt in the gloom, as eyes scanned frantically over the place where the dazzling light had been.

In the darkness, the man with the broken nose breathed heavily, still clutching Davies' baton as he whirled around, trying to work out where their quarry had gone. He didn't have to wait long.

Something closed firmly around his wrist, and before he had a chance to react, something else hit him hard in the kidneys. He staggered to his knees and released the baton in surprise.

In the darkness, Jess Layton stood holding her torch in one hand, and the Sergeant's baton in the other.

'I'll take that,' she muttered to the groaning figure who was now trying to clamber upright, eyes whipping frantically around as he tried to see his mysterious assailant. Then she clicked the beam back on, brought the baton down hard on his shoulder, and the fight began.

A snarling man launched himself straight at the torch beam, and Jess admired his tenacity before she brought the upswing of her baton around to crunch heavily into his jaw. As he dropped back, howling in pain, a huge man in a dirty tracksuit thumped hard into her from behind. Jess staggered forwards, torch beam swinging wildly up towards the towering ceiling.

The whirling light distracted her opponents for a moment, and she shoved outwards, her arms connecting with grubby sweatshirts and rough army surplus jackets as she thrust bodies frantically away from her space. Heavy boots thumped into the floor as men staggered backwards into the bodies rushing up behind them, and Jess found a gap just large enough to duck between flailing limbs and shove out towards the opposite stairs of the mezzanine.

Then the gunfire started.

The muzzle of a shotgun exploded in the darkness, and suddenly the barn was full of panicked voices as pellets sprayed into the crowd. A gaunt man with a mop of greasy, dark hair had made it to the top of the metal stairs on the other wall of the barn, brandishing one of the weapons from the crates below. As he went to pull the trigger again, the huge tattooed man beside him grabbed the muzzle in one massive hand and shoved it roughly towards the floor.

'What the fuck you even firing at, Derek?' the tattooed man grunted, squinting into the chaotic darkness on the mezzanine.

'The torch, you prick,' his greasy companion snarled back, wrestling the gun free and looking over at the stairs that led up from the opposite side of the barn, where a skinny young man in oversized designer jeans had just crested the top. He stood in a faint shaft of dusty light, which illuminated the barrel of the pistol that he gripped nervously in both hands. It shook a little as he aimed at the yelling crowd.

'Aim at the torch!' the greasy man shouted, and the young pistol-gripper nodded, eyes wide in the darkness, and fired.

Blood bloomed on the army surplus jacket of a tall man who stood behind Jess. He bellowed in pain as he realised the pistol's bullet had pierced his side. The tall man staggered backwards, colliding with Jess, and for a moment her concentration dropped as his now bloody hand slapped into her from behind.

The torch and baton went clattering to the floor as she temporarily forgot how to grip their solid forms.

Swearing, she thrust out her hands for them, just as the greasy man's shotgun rang out again, aiming for the torch as it fell. The frantically churning bodies on the mezzanine stampeded away from the gunmen on each staircase, converging in the centre in a great tangle of panicked limbs.

The shooting stopped as the gunmen lost their target in the chaos. Jess was knocked forwards onto her knees, eyes desperately hunting for the flashes of light in between heavy boots and gleaming trainers. She felt legs beginning to press in on every side of her.

No one could see her as she was crushed between them, and the huge man in the dirty tracksuit suddenly fell as his legs collided with Jess, thrown unexpectedly off balance. His weight plunged down on to her, and Jess found herself trapped between him and the rough boards that formed the floor of the mezzanine.

She began to panic, her brain in disarray. She couldn't move upwards through the solid human spirits around her, she couldn't move sideways – could she let herself fall through the floor? What would happen if she fell? How could she stop herself being solid, when every single spectral cell of her was so completely convinced that she was bring crushed to death?

Then something skittered towards her, and her eyes widened. The baton had rolled towards her hand, and she grabbed for it amongst the pounding chaos of feet. Jess seized it and used her remaining inches of movement to ram it upwards, straight into the neck of the huge man on top of her.

He let out a groan and rolled sideways, unbalancing bodies like bowling pins as his weight hit the crush of panicking people now beginning to scatter again.

As her body came free of his bulk, Jess took a great shuddering breath, and saw her torch beam emerge between the dispersing tangle of legs. She scrambled to her knees and lunged forwards, closing her hands around the small plastic barrel and pulling herself shakily upright.

As she did so, she felt another hand grasp the torch, and looked up into the face of the man with the broken nose. His expression was strange, contorted in confusion, as he tried to make sense of the seemingly floating object in front of him.

Jess took advantage of his consternation and raised the fist which still gripped the baton, before thrusting it hard into his nose. As her hand connected with the broken cartilage, she felt it crunch sickeningly under her knuckles, and a fresh spray of blood spurted from the bruised mess in the centre of his face.

He yelled in agony and staggered backwards, clearing the last knot of people away from Jess's position, leaving her standing momentarily alone.

Jess realised that she was now stood in a dusty beam of light, which poured onto the mezzanine from a window that had been set too high in the wall to be barricaded. On the astral plane, it looked as though her blue-hued body was glowing in the light, catching the police insignia on her stab vest and making her polished boots shine.

To her opponents, it was increasingly clear that they were looking at a floating torch and baton.

For a long moment, nobody moved. Then Jess heard a soft rustle as the greasy man raised his shotgun, the muzzle aimed straight at her. Instinctively, she gripped her torch and baton and ran forwards, weapon raised, concentrating on keeping her grip, even as the shotgun roared again.

She realised as she was about to reach him that the gunman had frozen, and was now staring in horror at a point somewhere around her torso. Jess looked down and saw that a small halo of pellets was embedded smokily into her stab vest.

To the gunman stood before her, pellets and shrapnel were now hanging in the air in front of him, held up inside whatever invisible figure currently clutched the weapon now inches from his face.

In shock, Jess staggered backwards, hands reaching instinctively for her torso. As she did so, she felt the objects tumble from her grasp again, and a rain of pellets clattered to the floor. Her mind raced, and she swore her stomach felt like it was on fire.

She remembered in that moment what Danny had told her in the gym - her body might not really be injured, but she was going to have a hell of a job convincing her mind that was the case.

Unfortunately, it was too late to worry about the consequences, as the tiny pieces of metal cascaded around her boots.

She dimly realised that the greasy man was running back down the stairs, and the rest of the group were charging the other way, running hard for the opposite staircase and pouring out onto the barn floor. She looked down at the still silent figure of Davies, lying alone, and took a deep breath before swinging herself off the balcony and dropping to the floor.

Jess fumbled the landing and hit the dusty floor hard. It knocked the wind out of her, as she wondered wildly again what damage she was doing to herself. She just couldn't seem to understand how to choose her solidity properly, and her astral mind kept telling her that every part of her body was now on fire with pain.

She staggered to her feet and towards Davies, as thundering steps came closer in the dark. She grabbed for a nearby metal chair and hurled it at the closest shadowy opponent, who broke his course as the metal legs thumped hard into his chest. He began to sprint for the door instead.

Jess grabbed for a beam of wood and flung that the other way, taking out the legs of the young man with the pistol as he scrambled past her. He crawled a few steps, the filth of the barn now smearing his designer jeans, before getting to his knees and following the other figure as it retreated rapidly for the door.

Two men diligently lunged forwards out of the darkness, trying to grab for the Sergeant's body as they fled. With the last of her strength, Jess delivered a firm uppercut to one, before launching a heavy kick to the stomach of the other.

All around her, feet were beating a heavy retreat, leaving her standing over the Sergeant. She was relieved to see he was still breathing, although his breaths seemed shallow and rapid as he lay motionless in a pool of his own blood.

In the chaos, Jess suddenly heard a familiar sound, and felt a rush of relief at the piercing scream of sirens surrounding the building. Shouts from outside told her that the cavalry had arrived, and her opponents were running into the not-so-loving arms of the Huntshire Police Force.

She took one last look at Davies, and then staggered swiftly out of the back wall, to where her slumped body still lurked behind the barn.

A few seconds later, Jess let herself in through the back door and flipped the switch inside the fuse box. Fluorescent lights blinked back to life, and in the sudden brightness, she saw that there was one figure unaccounted for.

Charlie Benson stood near the Sergeant's body, peering terrified into the corners of the barn around him. He whirled to look at Jess as she approached, his eyes wide and panicked. She felt a small flicker of smugness as his gaze locked onto her, and his eyes grew wider still. Jess trod carefully towards him, pulling her cuffs from her belt.

'What the fuck was that?' he panted, and she tried to suppress a smile as she stopped in front of him. Charlie's eyes narrowed. 'You're limping,' he observed slowly, and Jess winced a little as her body provided her with a fresh surge of pain. Despite not seeming to have a scratch on her, her brain was determined to remind her that she'd technically just been shot and dropped from a first-floor mezzanine.

'It seems there's a lot you don't know about the Huntshire Police Force,' Jess told Charlie, as she folded her arms and watched the large man seem to wilt under her gaze. 'Just remember that, next time you threaten one of our officers.'

Charlie nodded dumbly, watching her with a mix of fascination and horror.

'Now then. Are you going to come quietly?' Jess asked him, and he reached out his hands mutely to accept the cuffs.

Jess clipped the cuffs firmly closed.

She yanked Charlie around by the shoulder of his expensive coat and marched him out of the barn, taking one last look at the Sergeant. Jess fervently hoped the medical team would be able to get in quickly, as soon as she confirmed the barn was empty.

As she stepped out into the bright sunlight, a strange hush passed over the scene, as dozens of faces turned to watch her hustle Charlie Benson through the doors of the barn. Eyes watched her from the back seats of police cars, from officers holding their detainees on the hoods of their vehicles, and from the waiting firearms team who rushed in to sweep the building as Jess nodded them through the doors.

A little way back, behind the cluster of cars and people, Jess saw Danny. He was also watching her as she hauled her prisoner across the rustling grass, but she couldn't read his expression at all.

15

Walking back through the corridors of the police station was a fantastic feeling. As Jess strode across the polished tiles, curious faces appeared from doorways, and officers walking past would turn to smile and watch her as she passed.

A cluster of firearms officers lumbered by, and their massive heads nodded in recognition as Jess grinned. The word had spread like wildfire, and once news had come back that the Sergeant was stable, the mood in the station was nothing short of jubilant.

Even better, it seemed that little could be got from any of their detainees beyond a shaky 'no comment'. Jess was quietly glad that Charlie Benson's strict rule on not talking to the police would keep her supernatural activities under wraps, for now.

The clean-up from the barn had been a huge scramble, but Jess had missed most of it while being checked for injuries. The medics had been very concerned by her internal pain, since they were struggling to find many outward signs of injury, but Jess finally managed to bat them away and join her team as they got the epic piles of paperwork underway.

She opened the doors to their office, to find the weary B Shift inside. They beamed as she entered, and she found herself beaming back as a hot cup of tea was thrust into her hand.

'Seriously, Jess, I don't know how you did it,' Grant told her enthusiastically, 'but the Sergeant's family called, and… oh, Jess, honestly, I'm so proud of you.' Jess noticed that Grant's eyes looked a bit misty, and Jess gave the diminutive officer a grateful nod.

'Thanks Grant,' she said, as Packer clapped a large arm around Jess's shoulders.

'Jess, darling, I would normally point out that you have committed a fucking excellent combination of Sections 13 *and* 15 of our beloved Cake Act - but quite frankly, I'm going to buy them on your behalf, you fucking diamond,' Packer bellowed affectionately, and Jess laughed.

'Thanks for the offer, but out of respect for our sacred Cake Act, I will buy them,' Jess confirmed, and Packer nodded sagely.

'Can I just point out to you all,' piped up Einstein, who was still grinning happily over at her from behind his habitually smeary glasses, 'that I will not only taking the fittest officer on our shift out for a drink - no offence ladies - but she's now also a literal shift hero. Long may she remain thoroughly out of my league,' he continued, and winked at Jess.

'Oh God, Einstein, I totally forgot that was tonight,' Jess gasped. 'Just give me a few minutes to get changed, I'm still a total mess.'

'Jess, quite frankly, when you walked out of that barn - I don't think you've ever looked better,' he said sincerely, and Jess blushed as her shift erupted into mocking noises. None of them noticed as Danny slunk back into the office, grabbed his bag, and quietly left.

As Jess was gathering her things to leave, the door swung back open, and there was a gentle hint of hairspray as the A Shift arrived, gleaming as usual. This time, they paused to watch Jess as she crossed the office, heading for the door.

'Hey, Packer,' one of the constables called as Jess approached, 'I think I need to change my bet. I'll give her another month, long enough to see if that was a massive fucking fluke.'

'Oh sorry,' Jess told him coolly as she passed, 'did no one tell you? All bets are off.'

The office door banged shut behind her, and Jess grinned as she heard the sound of B Shift bellowing with delight through the door.

*

A few minutes later, Jess emerged from the changing rooms in a simple red dress and flats, her bag slung over one shoulder. She had managed to brush the day's mess out of her hair and attempted to cover up the tiredness on her face with a little make-up.

As she headed down the corridor, she realised Einstein was waiting there for her, looking uncharacteristically smart in an ironed shirt and trousers. He grinned when he saw her.

'I take it back, Jess, you look even lovelier now,' he told her as she approached him, and she flushed a little.

'You know, I'm really looking forward to this,' she told him as they swung into step down the corridor.

'Well shit, no pressure then,' he joked, and she laughed.

'Jess!' a voice called suddenly, and they turned back to see Danny standing at the other end of the corridor. He walked towards them, taking in their clothes and frowning.

'Where are you going?' Danny asked warily, eyeing Einstein's unusually neat shirt.

'Einstein is taking me for a drink,' Jess replied cautiously, and Danny snorted slightly.

'Sure. Well… have fun. You still need somewhere to stay?' Danny asked Jess bluntly, as Einstein raised his eyebrows in mild surprise.

'That would actually be great… if that's still alright?' Jess asked awkwardly, realising it would be difficult at this point to retract her previous night's excuse. 'I, um, I'm having some problems with my new place,' Jess explained to Einstein, who still looked a little bemused. 'Danny kindly offered that I could use his sofa. Just haven't had time to get it fixed yet,' she finished lamely.

'So, Jess, my grandmother's going to be home this evening,' Danny continued, ignoring Einstein completely. 'She's very keen to meet you.'

'Oh, wow, right,' Jess said, feeling a little bewildered. 'I didn't realise - I mean, we might be quite late...'

'No problem,' Danny assured her. 'We'll wait up.'

'Shall we get going?' Einstein asked, his eyebrows furrowed as he watched Danny warily. Jess nodded.

'I'll see you later, Danny,' she told her tutor, as she and Einstein turned to head back down the corridor.

'Bring her back in one piece, Einstein,' Danny called after them, and Jess looked briefly back over her shoulder, to see him watching them carefully as they left.

'You know,' Einstein told her conspiratorially as they walked, 'I do, in fact, have a real name. It may astonish you to know that my parents, in their infinite wisdom, christened me Max,' he said, and Jess grinned.

'I think I prefer Einstein,' she told him wryly, and he grimaced.

'So do I,' he agreed, and the two of them walked in step together, across the station's busy reception, and out into the dark car park.

*

Hours later, Jess's face still hurt slightly from laughing as they walked together down the pavement that led to Danny's quiet street. Their shadows swung from streetlight to streetlight, and Jess pulled her arms tighter around herself to guard against the slight summer breeze that ruffled the bushes as they passed.

The sweet evening smell of flowers hung in the air, but every now and again Jess caught a faint wisp of Einstein's aftershave as they walked, often close enough that their shoulders brushed affectionately as they headed towards the dark row of houses.

They had certainly raised plenty of glasses to her successful arrest that night, and Jess's feet stumbled a little as Einstein gestured his way enthusiastically through an anecdote.

Their shoes scrunched to a halt on the gravel path that led to the bungalow, and Jess turned to smile at her companion as he looked nervously down at her, the yellow glow of the streetlights reflected in his glasses.

'So, um, you know that I also have a sofa?' he asked her suddenly, and blushed as Jess's eyebrows shot upwards. 'Sorry. I don't mean that in a weird way, just - you know, if you're stuck for somewhere to stay.'

Jess smiled ruefully up at him and shook her

head.

'Thanks for the offer, but hopefully I'll be home soon anyway.'

'If you're sure... I'll even let you meet *my* nan, if you want,' Einstein joked, and Jess laughed as the door behind them swung open.

More golden light spilled out onto the path, as Danny stood framed in the bungalow's doorway. Einstein glanced up at him, then turned to look at Jess again.

'So... uh, good night?' he offered awkwardly, and Jess smiled.

'Night, Max,' she told him quietly, and then reached up, placing her hand on his shoulder and pulling herself gently towards him, planting a soft kiss on one cheek. She felt his breath brush warmly against her face as he grinned, and she grinned back.

Then she turned and walked away up the path, to where Danny stood waiting, his face in shadow. As she approached, she noticed he was looking over her shoulder, watching Einstein as he sloped away up the dark pavement.

'So. Ready to meet my grandmother?' he asked Jess, and she nodded nervously.

'I think so,' she told him, trying her best to think sober thoughts.

Danny stepped back to let Jess squeeze past him into the hallway, before closing the door behind her with a snap and a heavy waft of sage.

16

As Danny ushered Jess into the dining room, she was suddenly grateful that she'd dressed up a little that evening.

The woman who stood by the tall sash windows was elegantly draped in a well-fitted green dress, with heavy gold jewellery that glinted softly in the warm lamplight of the dining room. Although her face was lightly lined, it was almost impossible to place her age in the dim room.

She turned as they entered, and Jess suddenly wondered whether the woman had been watching as she said goodbye to Einstein on the path. Something about that idea didn't make her feel entirely comfortable.

'You must be Jess,' the woman announced, moving effortlessly forwards, and extending an elegant hand. Jess reached out awkwardly to take it, not sure whether her host intended a handshake, and was then pulled in suddenly for a delicate kiss on the cheek.

The older woman's perfume was disturbed in the air between them, and Jess realised there was just the tiniest hint of sage in the floral blend. Clearly Danny's grandmother didn't like her work to follow her around.

'And I'm Rita,' the woman purred as Jess pulled away, before turning towards her grandson. 'Tea, if you wouldn't mind, Daniel,' she instructed him, seating herself at the dining table with a gentle rattle of jewellery.

Danny clumped away towards the kitchen, and after a moment, there came the sound of a boiling kettle. Jess hovered awkwardly for a moment by the table, but then Rita reached out her hand again, gesturing to the chair opposite.

'Please,' she invited, and Jess perched dutifully on the chair, as Rita studied her carefully across the delicately crocheted tablecloth.

'Now, then. I don't have long, but I insisted I had to meet you,' Rita began warmly. 'My grandson hasn't had a tutee before, in his day job, I mean. Well, he definitely hasn't had one here, either!' she laughed, and Jess realised that the warmth in Rita's voice definitely didn't extend as far as her eyes. Jess shifted uncomfortably on her chair, subconsciously trying to sit up straighter.

'I understand you've been introduced to projecting a little… sooner than planned,' Rita continued, and Jess stiffened. The edge in the older woman's voice was clear now, and after a moment, Jess took a deep breath and leaned forwards into the lamp-light.

'Look. I'm assuming Danny has told you a reasonable amount about - well, about everything that's happened. I know you probably think I've been pretty irresponsible, but I promise you, I'm not taking any of this lightly,' Jess insisted, as Rita raised one immaculately groomed eyebrow at her.

'Oh, I certainly didn't think you were taking it lightly,' she countered, leaning back slightly in her own chair and continuing to study Jess carefully. 'Daniel's been known to run off for the odd solo adventure too,' she added, as Danny re-entered the room, carrying a tray containing three steaming cups of tea.

Jess noticed that instead of their usual mugs, her tutor had chosen proper china cups and saucers, their rims daintily decorated with a floral motif that clashed enthusiastically with every other print in the room. Rita barely looked around as hers was set down in front of her, but Jess glanced up at Danny as he handed her a cup, before seating himself between them.

'Still,' Rita said, raising her tea and sipping grace-fully, 'at least no one was hurt.'

'Well, technically I did get shot,' Jess joked weakly, and Danny stared at her in alarm.

'You didn't tell me you got shot,' he hissed, and Jess shrugged awkwardly.

'I mean, I wasn't shot in the actual body, just the… astral one,' Jess explained, gesturing vaguely at her midriff. 'It's OK, it just really hurts every now and again.'

'Good to see it didn't stop you going out this evening,' Rita commented, taking another sip of her tea. Jess hesitated, watching the other woman's expression carefully. It was difficult to read behind the delicate china teacup, but Jess got the distinct feeling that asking Einstein to walk her to the bungalow might have been an error.

'I mean, it was arranged before I... got shot,' Jess explained uncomfortably, and the table fell into silence. Jess reached for her own tea, grateful for something to do with her hands. She wasn't used to drinking tea with a proper cup and saucer, and the china clinked loudly as she awkwardly set her cup back down.

'So. You must have a lot of questions,' Rita said eventually, and as Danny leaned forwards to look at Jess, she was reminded distinctly of her last job interview. She shifted nervously again, racking her brain for a sensible question.

'Do you know other people who do this?' Jess asked slowly, and Rita smiled slightly. It seemed this was indeed a sensible question.

'We do. There are very few people in this country who actually practice the services we offer, though plenty will tell you they do. We like to keep a close handle on any genuine practitioners. So, there is an... organisation that I belong to, which regulates the field.'

Jess raised her eyebrows and noticed that Danny

was now concentrating on his tea.

'Are you part of this organisation too?' she asked him quietly, and he looked up at her, his expression hard to read as he shook his head stiffly.

'Generally, as we practice together, there's no need for us to both be members, although naturally I hope Daniel might take my position if I... retire,' Rita told Jess smoothly. 'For now, my main concern is to ensure Daniel continues to project safely, with a good partner.'

She was watching Jess carefully again now, and with a considerable amount of wine still coursing through her veins, Jess found herself returning the stare with a surprising amount of boldness.

'So, you don't mind that he recruited me while you were away?' Jess asked bluntly, and noticed her tutor glance up at her sharply. Rita's smile widened, but for the first time, Jess thought she actually looked quite pleased.

'I suppose I broadly expected something like this to happen, sooner or later,' she replied, finishing the last of her tea and setting the cup down carefully. 'Although when he told me he'd recruited his partner, I didn't realise he actually meant his... police colleague.'

'So, is it usual, for people to recruit their... "partners"?' Jess asked cautiously.

'Oh, I certainly brought a couple of my husbands into the fold, for a while,' Rita told her, leaning back into the lamplight, chin propped on one elegant hand. 'But we do have a strict limit on how many

187

people we like to see practising at one time, so... I do hope you weren't hoping to involve your boyfriend, Jess,' she added, and Jess glanced at Danny again. She was surprised to see that he was now watching her carefully too.

'Um, that wasn't actually – I mean, he's just another one of my colleagues, but it literally hadn't occurred to me, so... no,' Jess offered awkwardly, and Rita nodded.

'Good. Although a word to the wise, if you were thinking that he might become more than "just another one of your colleagues",' Rita paused, her lip curling slightly, 'you'll generally find it doesn't go down too well, when you need to keep disappearing into the night with another man. Just something to think about,' she purred, as a grandfather clock in the corner began to chime midnight.

Rita turned and gave it a casual glance, before casting one last sweeping stare over Jess.

'Bedtime, I think,' she announced, standing up in a gentle jingle of jewellery. 'I'm sure that if you have more questions, they can wait until I return,' she added, as Jess and Danny both clambered to their feet.

'Wait, are you going again?' Danny asked, and for a moment Jess thought her tutor suddenly seemed younger, as he gazed across the dining table at his grandmother.

'I need to be on a flight early, so I may not see you before I leave, but it seems like you have things largely under control,' she told him, and Jess noticed that her smile for Danny seemed more genuine. 'Goodnight, Daniel. A pleasure to meet you, Jess,' she added, as she swept out of the room, leaving her empty teacup behind her on the table.

Danny moved forwards to begin tidying things away, and Jess picked up her own cup and saucer, setting them gently on the tray.

'Am I just really bad at first impressions?' Jess asked bluntly, and he looked up at her in surprise. After a long pause, Jess nodded to herself. 'Yeah. Great.'

'Look, I would definitely say I've liked you better as I've got to know you,' Danny told her uncomfortably, and Jess sighed.

'How diplomatic. You know, you could have warned me that your grandma was hoping we would hook up,' Jess told him sternly, and Danny's eyebrows shot towards the ceiling.

'I'm not sure that she was -'

'Oh please,' Jess interrupted, 'what else was all that about?'

'Well... she's not wrong,' he began awkwardly, and Jess leaned away from him as he moved towards her, edging around the table. 'It is easier, you know, seeing someone who actually knows what the hell you're doing with half your life.'

'Oh shit, Danny,' Jess said, shaking her head, 'please, tell me that's not what all this is about.'

They stood for a long moment in the dim dining room, and Jess recognised the soft, pleading look in her tutor's eyes as he gazed down at her. She backed

189

away, raising her hands.

'I'm sorry, Danny, but when I came to you, I honestly just needed your help. And I'm more than happy to help you in return, you know that. But that doesn't mean... do you see what I'm trying to say?' Jess asked him, noticing her voice had now taken on a pleading edge.

'Come on, Jess,' Danny said, moving forwards, and reaching out his hands towards her. 'I'm a nice guy, I know we didn't get off to the best start, but -'

'Danny, stop,' Jess said firmly, as she felt her back collide with a bookcase at the edge of the room. She felt something topple from the shelf behind her and hit the carpeted floor with a soft thump. Looking down, she realised with a thrill that it was the dagger, sitting innocently in its leather sheath.

'What happens if I decide I don't want to do this with you anymore?' Jess asked Danny quietly, and he frowned at her.

'What do you mean?'

'Your grandmother's 'organisation'... what happens if I want to stop doing this, but I already know about it?' Jess asked bluntly, and she saw Danny's eyes flicker away slightly as he considered his response. She nodded slowly.

'Right. Then consider this my... temporary resignation,' Jess told him carefully. 'Maybe you could hold off telling your grandmother just yet, give me a few days to properly think about it?'

Danny nodded slowly back.

'OK. Good. So, in that case, I think I'm going to

go home,' Jess told him firmly, and began to move past Danny, towards the open dining room door.

'Wait, Jess,' he called after her, moving forwards and catching her by the arm. As she turned back, Jess saw he had the pleading look back in his eyes, and she grimaced slightly as she tugged her arm away. 'What about the ghost?'

'The what? Oh shit, yeah,' Jess said, shaking her head slightly. Her head was still reeling from everything that had happened since she last left her house, to the point where she'd almost forgotten she would still be sharing her home with her unknown visitor.

'You know what? I'll sort something out. See you at work, Danny,' she told her tutor sadly, heading out of the dining room.

To Jess's relief, he didn't move to follow her this time, and she found herself glancing back down the bungalow's narrow hallway as she quietly left the front door, heading back out into the dark garden.

She couldn't see Rita Jackson anywhere as she left, but Jess reckoned a net curtain in the lounge might have twitched just a little, as her tired feet carried her back out into the night.

17

As she finally collapsed back into her own hallway, Jess kicked off her shoes, feeling distinctly agitated.

'Anyone home?' she called into the quiet house. 'Tap once for "yes"? Or flick a light, or whatever?'

She felt a little disappointed when nothing happened, and padded though to the kitchen, her mind churning slowly. There was still something needling at her, all the way back from that morning.

In the turmoil of the barn raid, the gunshots, her date with Einstein and meeting Danny's mysterious grandmother, Jess had almost forgotten that she had started her day with the news of Shane Wilson's untimely death.

Pulling her phone from her pocket, she brought up a local news site, tapping in searches, wondering if anything would come up.

Leaford news, Shane Wilson, suicide

No relevant results appeared, so Jess tried a different angle.

Leaford news, Faye Parker, suicide

This was a different story. Already, word was spreading, and Jess felt her stomach constrict as she read the testimonials already being dragged across multiple sites.

> *'lovely girl, so sad…'*
> *'so much to live for…'*
> *'so hard to understand…'*
> *'miss you so much…'*

Jess turned her phone screen away for a second, rubbing her eyes. She wondered fleetingly whether searching a police database would give her more of what she was actually looking for. The problem was that not only would that be a risk to her job, since she wasn't connected in any way to that particular case, but she also couldn't define exactly what she was trying to find.

After a moment, she tried another search.

Leaford news, Bill James, suicide

This time a news article arrived, and Jess scrolled through, until one particular phrase caught her eye.

'Bill, 48, had recently been acquitted of sexual assault…'

Her eyes narrowed as she studied the small screen. An idea was beginning to form in her mind, and as she mulled it over, it occurred to her that she wasn't sure where Bill James might currently be.

Musing on this, she absent-mindedly flicked on the kettle and the kitchen radio, then reached for a mug and a tea bag.

A familiar voice floated through the kitchen.

'Welcome back to the late show with me, Ricky White, getting you through the night. Coming up, I've got some rather strong feelings on yesterday's *Antiques Roadshow*, and I'll be sharing them with your delighted ears in just a moment. But first, my producer, in his infinite wisdom, has a new segment idea to share with you all…' Ricky drawled, as a cheaply produced jingle rang out.

The kettle finished boiling with a click, and Jess reached for it, pouring water deftly into her mug and watching it slowly colour as it brewed.

'Basically, the format works like this. You text in to the show, with a message that you want me to read to someone else who's also listening to the radio. Instead of, I don't know, texting them.

'So, yes. Please send me your delightful messages, to all your friends and acquaintances who for some godforsaken reason don't have their own bloody phone,' Ricky grumbled, and Jess suddenly frowned.

Picking up her phone again, she fired off a text, before fishing the tea bag from her mug and adding a dash of milk. After an experimental sip, Jess was quietly pleased. She was sure her tea-making skills were improving.

'Oh, bloody hell, we've actually got one,' Ricky sighed from the radio. 'Right. So, to some bloke called "Bill James", if you're lucky enough to be listening, a lady called Jess Layton says she wants to see you again tonight, in the warehouse. She will be coming alone, apparently. You know what, I'm going to play some adverts, this has already taken a sinister turn,' Ricky announced, and a commercial for double glazing began to play.

Heart thumping, Jess grinned a little to herself. There had definitely been a radio in the dusty corner of the warehouse, but she had no way of knowing if Bill played it to fill the long, lonely hours between shifts, or even whether he was still within five hundred miles of the building.

Jess took a moment to finish her tea, savouring the taste and the feeling of warm steam against her face. As she felt the hot liquid surge through her body, giving her an extra jolt of energy, she plonked her mug back down onto the kitchen side.

Then she strode back into her hallway, found her black kit bag, and fished out another small glass bottle.

As Jess strode into the dark, brooding interior of the warehouse, she was struck by how little had really changed. Maybe some boxes had moved a little, maybe the stock was slightly altered, but largely it seemed like life had continued steadily on without the warehouse manager who had dangled from the balcony all those days ago.

As she gazed about her astral self, peering into the deep, blue-black shadows, Jess tried to work out if the knot in her stomach was sympathy for the man she had found hanging here alone. Clearly, there was plenty about him she didn't understand - and her tutor hadn't felt the need to share.

More than anything, Jess felt an urge to ask questions. After all, what was she supposed to do, if not gather evidence?

Walking silently through the towering shelves of the warehouse, she watched each corner for signs of movement. As she glanced into a gap between skeletal metal shelving, she thought there was a flicker of motion in the darkness.

Pausing, she looked closer, but nothing emerged. Treading cautiously, she proceeded towards the area beneath the metal mezzanine, where the noose had hung over the cold concrete floor. She stepped into the deep shadows beneath the overhanging balcony, moving silently towards the area where a huge forklift loomed out of the dark, its metal catching the light with a bluish, astral glow.

Then something moved behind her, and she whirled around.

Bill James stood there, and for the first time, Jess properly registered that he still wore his work overalls, just as he had when she initially saw his spectral form.

He was eyeing her own police uniform with deep suspicion, and even as she watched, he seemed to back away slightly.

'Bill James?' she asked, and he nodded warily.

'Jess Layton?' he asked in turn, and she nodded back.

For a moment, the two spectres regarded each other carefully in the dark, both tensed and ready to move. Then Jess took a deep breath, raising her hands a little in supplication, trying to give Bill some kind of reassurance.

'It's OK, I really did come on my own. I need to ask you some questions.'

He nodded again, and Jess found herself glancing quickly over her own shoulder, mildly relieved that nothing else seemed to be emerging from the dark shelving.

'Right,' she continued, trying to organise her racing thoughts, 'I want to keep this quick. I don't know how long I've got, in case anyone else heard my radio message, so I'm going to get right to it. Bill, I need to know more about how you died.'

Bill started a little at her blunt tone, and his eyes also darted briefly around the dark space. Satisfied they were alone, Bill took a cautious step forwards.

'You know how I died, right? You saw my body,' he began slowly, and Jess nodded.

'Yeah, I did. The thing is, Bill... there's been a few bodies lately, and they're just not sitting right with me. I know this might be hard - but can you describe to me what actually happened when you died?' Jess asked.

Something about the pained grimace on Bill's face told her that she was definitely looking in the right place for answers.

'He said I shouldn't tell anyone,' Bill began miserably, and Jess reached out instinctively, grasping his arm.

'I thought you might say something like that,' she murmured reassuringly, letting go of his arm with a last, comforting pat. 'But I can't help you if I don't really understand what happened.'

Bill took a deep breath, and his eyes finally stopped flicking around the warehouse as he fixed her with a penetrating, desperate stare.

'I don't know exactly how it happened. I was on my own, locking up, and then suddenly - I don't know how to explain this, it was like a hand over my mouth, and then something... something was *in* my mouth, in my throat, and it tasted... I don't know,' he rambled, and Jess nodded encouragingly.

'Then I opened my eyes, and everything looked wrong,' he continued, his voice rising, growing more desperate. 'And I could see my own body there, on the floor... but then it got up, and it started walking, and talking, and it... I don't know, it was telling me all these things and then it took a rope and I watched it, I watched it…'

He trailed off, and Jess realised there were tears in his eyes. She hesitated, watching his face carefully in the dark.

'What was it saying to you, exactly?' she asked slowly.

'It knew,' Bill said miserably. 'It knew what I did.'

'What did you do?' Jess pressed him, feeling herself leaning slightly away from the other spirit as she did so.

'She worked here,' he continued bluntly. 'She was sweet… I don't care what anybody says, she was asking for it.'

'Asking for what?' Jess whispered, her tone like ice.

'You fucking know,' Bill snarled suddenly, and Jess felt her body tense as she tried to gauge his expression, trying to find the fine line between a human scowl and the wild, animal stare of Terry Haines. 'You work with him, don't you? Why are you even here?'

'I don't know, that's exactly why I'm here,' Jess snapped, but as Bill spoke, her blood ran cold with the thrill of realisation. 'I want you to tell me.'

'After I watched myself die,' Bill cried, 'he was here. In this fucking warehouse. He told me it was the only way he could get me. So, you lot fucking win. Are you happy?' he yelled, and this time Jess thought she saw more than a human snarl on his face.

Her training kicking in, Jess's forearm flew up to block as Bill lunged forwards, and as she saw his hand whirl around for a blow, she raised one spectral knee and thumped him right in the stomach.

He doubled over her leg, and the animal bellow died from his throat as he slumped to the ground.

'Come to finish me off, then?' he gasped, as Jess backed away from where he crouched pathetically on the floor.

'No,' she told him bluntly, staring down at him. 'You know, I actually came to deliver a bit of justice. The justice, in fact, was for you, though maybe you don't deserve it. Because you want to know how "our lot" win? We win by the law, not by whatever bollocks this was.'

Bill stared up at her in mild terror as Jess drew herself up and took a final deep breath.

'Just tell me. Who did you see?' she asked, and Bill's eyes widened.

'The officer. His name's Jackson, yeah. PC Jackson,' he told her, and Jess felt all the tension in her body rush to a sudden knot in her gut. She stood for a long moment, looking out into the darkness around her, until Bill spoke again.

'What are you going to do to me?' he moaned, still crouching in the shadows. Jess paused, staring down at him.

'Well,' she began finally, 'that depends on what you decide. If you feel some remorse for what you've done, and you genuinely want to be finished with all this… I want you to go and find Leaford Psychic Services, 59 Tallis Road. They'll finish the job, and you can move on.

'You want to keep wandering about? Fine. But if I ever hear about you touching another hair on someone's head,' Jess murmured, treading slowly forwards, 'I will personally come and find you. And let me put it this way. I'm what's coming, for what killed you.'

Bill shrank away from her boots as she came to a stop, looming over him. Then he scrambled away, crawling, then running, disappearing through a shelf, then a wall, away into the night.

As she stood alone, in between metal shelves that stretched away into the gloom above, Jess's eyes burned bright in the darkness. Behind her, a shadow flickered in a dim corridor of boxes, unseen and unheard.

18

After a long, exhausted night's sleep, Jess awoke to an unfamiliar smell wafting up the stairs. She sniffed for a few moments, before her tired brain finally realised that it smelt like smoke.

As the fire alarm kicked into gear, Jess launched herself upright and crashed out onto the landing. She felt a remarkable sense of déjà vu as she stood framed in the bedroom doorway, with the hair on her head piled untidily from sleep, and the hair on her arms standing on end.

Jess pounded down the stairs and into the kitchen, where she found nothing more dramatic than a little smoke wafting gently from her cheap plastic toaster. Grabbing a tea towel, she frantically beat the smoke away from the alarm, and the beeping finally died.

Moving back over to the toaster, Jess discovered that someone had extracted two slices of bread from a hastily bought bag of supplies, which was mostly still sitting unpacked on the kitchen counter. The kettle was also steaming hot, with just enough water inside for a single brew.

Jess looked over her shoulder at the empty kitchen.

'Am I right in assuming that ghosts can't eat?' she asked, and a teaspoon hovered gently into the air next to her. It gave a single, ringing tap against a jar of spaghetti.

'Right. So, you made breakfast for me?' Jess checked, as she threw a tea bag into a mug, and piled the slightly charred toast onto a plate.

The teaspoon tapped once.

'You're the best,' Jess laughed, padding over to the fridge to find butter for her toast.

Behind her, the teaspoon tapped once again.

When her breakfast was assembled, Jess carefully carried everything through to the living room, and sat down in her usual, comfortable spot on the sofa. She noticed that once again, the ghost seemed to settle on the cushion next to her.

Jess took a warming, soothing sip of tea, and then carefully set down the mug, looking over at the seemingly empty space beside her.

'So. There's something I did want to talk to you about,' she began awkwardly, and she felt for a moment as though the gap next to her seemed more expectant.

'The thing is,' Jess continued, 'I really do want to meet you properly. But there's a slight complication.

When I left the other evening, I was going to get more… supplies. Sorry - I'm still not really sure how much of the detail I should tell you, it feels a bit like "classified" information, I suppose? And I'm supposed to be quite good at not leaking that, generally speaking, with my day job…'

Jess sighed and stuffed some comforting toast into her mouth.

'Anyway. My point is, I would really like to meet you properly, but I'm going to have limited opportunities to… well, to project, which is the only way I can actually see you. And I don't mean to sound like a massive dick, but maybe it would be more efficient if we could therefore tie that in with me doing something else? Ah, wow. Did I sound like a massive dick?'

Jess noticed that the pencil on the coffee table had risen into the air again, but it was hesitating.

'So, I don't mean to lead your answer,' she joked weakly, 'but maybe as well as tapping once for "yes", we could agree on tapping twice for "no"?'

After a long pause, the pencil gently tapped twice.

'Sorry,' Jess grimaced. 'Thanks for breakfast.'

Just then, Jess's phone pinged loudly, and she jumped a little. Leaning forwards, she read the name on the incoming message, and a smile instinctively twitched the corner of her mouth.

EINSTEIN 09:34
Hey Jess. Have super important follow up to my

excellent story about crabs. Fancy hearing the sequel over coffee? x

'You know,' Jess mused as she picked up her phone and fired off a reply, 'I haven't told you about my rather exciting twenty-four hours out of the house! So, not only did I arrest an actual, legitimate gangster, getting literally shot in the process, but I also went on a date. It may have been my greatest Thursday yet.'

Her phone pinged again, and Jess glanced down at the reply.

EINSTEIN 09:36
Great! Are you back at your place then? I'll pop over in about an hour? I'll bring the cake ;) x

Jess grinned to herself and fired off a perky *'Yup! That sounds great! x'*.

She took a deep breath, then looked around her cluttered living room and down at her untidy pyjamas. Her face, almost entirely bereft of make-up other than the remnants of badly-cleansed mascara, fell.

'Oh shit, no,' Jess breathed, and launched herself off the sofa towards the stairs, the shower, and her limited stock of cleaning supplies.

*

An hour later, as Jess opened her front door to Einstein's warm smile, she tried to look nonchalantly like the kind of well-groomed, well-dressed individual whose house always achieved a certain level of tasteful minimalism.

She reckoned that if the hallway cupboard could keep holding the groaning weight of her assorted possessions, she might just get away with it.

'Jesus, Jess, you look far too perky for a police officer on a rest day,' Einstein grinned, and Jess blushed happily back at him. He held up his left hand, in which he brandished a boxed red velvet cake.

'Sainsbury's Finest, for Huntshire's finest,' he offered, holding it out to her.

'Thanks,' Jess laughed, taking it and leading him into the house. He wiped his feet carefully and nodded politely around at her hallway.

'Nice place. Shall I pop the kettle on?' he asked, and Jess turned back to him, grinning.

'Do you literally not trust me to make tea in my own home?' she asked, and he shrugged.

'I'm not sure I trust you to make tea anywhere, probie,' he told her, winking. 'But tell you what, I'll make the tea and teach you to do the paperwork, and you can get on with fighting gangsters in barns. We all have our talents,' he said sincerely, and Jess laughed again as she led him into the kitchen.

The kettle boiled and Jess decanted the cake onto a plate, as Einstein blundered about in her unfamiliar kitchen, trying to be helpful. They kept colliding in the small space as Jess pointed out where things were kept, and she quietly smiled to herself every time he brushed his hand against hers.

'So, you mentioned teaching me to do paper-work,' she said eventually. 'Does that mean you want to take me out on shift again?'

'Yeah, I'd honestly love to,' Einstein told her earnestly, 'I'm thinking of becoming a tutor now, actually. I mean, you're my first ever probie and you're already turning out great, so clearly I'd be the bollocks,' he insisted, taking a big sip of tea and trying to keep a straight face.

Jess totally failed to keep hers straight as he eyed her over the rim of his mug, which announced to the kitchen in a large red font that its drinker was 'Fucking Fabulous'.

'I'd like that,' she told him, and he beamed. 'I mean, I assume it's OK for me to do some shifts with someone other than Danny? Even if he's not on leave?'

'Yeah, I think so,' Einstein mused, 'I definitely went out with a couple of officers to start with. Look, Jess, I don't mean to sound like an arse, but... I just don't really know if Danny's got his heart in it - the tutoring, I mean. And I really do think you've got something in you - you massively turned it around, you know? Maybe it wouldn't be the worst thing if you tried shaking things up a bit, spend time with some different officers?'

Jess nodded eagerly. Spending time with some-one other than Danny sounded like a pretty fantastic idea right now, and she smiled encouragingly at Einstein as he peered anxiously at her over his steaming tea.

'You know what? Let's ask when we get back. See if we can get some shifts double crewed together,' she told him, and he beamed.

They both reached for plates of red velvet cake and began to tuck in eagerly.

'So, what's been going wrong with this place?' Einstein asked, and Jess frowned.

'What do you mean?'

'I thought there was something that needed fixing, that's why you were staying with Danny?' Einstein clarified, now frowning back at Jess.

'Oh… yeah, bit of an embarrassing one, actually. Turns out, I did not know where the fuse box was. So, it's… fixed, I guess?' Jess said, laughing. After a moment, Einstein laughed too, although Jess noticed that his frown still lingered.

'Um, just to be really clear on this,' Jess explained carefully, 'I did literally think there wasn't any power in the house, before I found the fuse box. I wasn't staying with Danny for… any other reason.'

'Right. No. Absolutely,' Einstein nodded awk-wardly. 'I mean, to be fair, you've got every right to… well, what I'm trying to say is, we've only actually been for a drink, and if you did want to stay with another bloke, you absolutely can do that…' he trailed off uncomfortably, and Jess noticed he had a bit of cream cheese icing on his nose from the red velvet cake. Without thinking, she reached up and brushed it off for him.

'Seriously, I have been staying on the sofa. Although duly noted, I think maybe staying there has been giving... a few people the wrong impression,' Jess mused, and Einstein nodded, watching her carefully.

'I mean,' he started cautiously, 'not that I want to give you the wrong impression either, but you can genuinely stay with me, if you ever want to, while you get things sorted out in your new place? I know it can feel a bit lonely when you're on your own, and you've got to figure out how everything works, and if something breaks... I mean, I've been there and it's rubbish. So, if you ever need it, I've got a sofa, you know?'

Jess smiled warmly at him, finishing the last of her cake and setting the plate down.

'I really appreciate that,' she began, and then without warning, her plate crashed loudly to the floor. Jess jumped backwards in alarm. She was sure her hand had been a good foot away from the plate when it tumbled.

'Shit, I must have knocked it,' she muttered frantically, reaching for the shards. Einstein set down his own plate and began reaching to help.

With another crash, his plate hit the laminate, also cracking sharply down the middle.

'Fuck, Jess, I'm sorry!' Einstein yelled in alarm, then frowned. 'I swear, I thought I just -'

The kitchen door banged loudly, making them both whirl around.

'Ah. Um, I do get some really strong breezes in here, actually,' Jess babbled nervously, sweeping the broken pieces of plate into her hands and piling them haphazardly onto the kitchen counter.

She looked up and noticed that just behind Einstein, a teaspoon hovered just next to the jar of pasta.

'I - I think maybe you should go,' Jess said hesitantly, and the spoon tapped once, lightly, against the jar. Einstein looked around, but the spoon was now lying innocently on the counter again.

'Sorry? Is everything OK?' he asked, bewildered. 'Is this because I asked you to stay? I really wasn't trying to be… I mean, I'm sorry. That must have come out the wrong way.'

He looked genuinely hurt, and Jess felt terrible, but she could see out of the corner of her eye that the spoon had risen quietly into the air again. She wasn't keen on Einstein staying around to meet her houseguest, especially if it led to an uncomfortable explanation to the Jacksons about why her 'boy-friend' was suddenly an expert in the supernatural.

'I'm sorry. I'll see you at work,' she said firmly, and Einstein opened his mouth to object. 'Look I'll - um, I'll explain then. Or I'll try to. I'm sorry,' she said again, shaking her head defeatedly.

Einstein nodded slowly, then turned to slope out of the kitchen. Jess saw him to the front door, and he turned back to give her one last puzzled frown.

'I, um, I'd still like to go out double crewed, if you

want to,' he offered, and Jess nodded, smiling sadly at him.

'Yeah. That would be great. Let's ask the Sergeant on Monday,' Jess told him. For a moment, his happy grin flickered back.

'See you, Jess,' he told her, ambling away up her path with a final, disappointed glance back.

She closed the door and took a deep breath.

'Seriously. What the fuck was that?' she exploded, but nothing answered. 'Were you upset about him being here? Is there a maximum number of living beings you can put up with at one time or something? What is your problem?'

Silence still flowed through the house, and Jess felt her fists clench instinctively. She stomped across to the hallway cupboard, pulling out her black kit bag, which had been stuffed unceremoniously inside to prepare for Einstein's arrival.

Rifling through it, her fingers closed on one of the small bottles nestled inside. She pulled it out, and for a moment, she stood alone in her sunlit hallway, listening intently to the tiny creaks and groans of the house around her. Then she sat down against the wall, uncorked the bottle, and drank.

Walking through her own house on the astral plane was a surreal experience. Even in the daytime, the shadows pooled deeply, and the sunlight looked colder and bluer than usual. Jess trod silently across the floors of her now familiar rooms, eyes flicking into every corner, looking for any hint of movement.

Nothing emerged.

As she walked, Jess's brain turned over and over, trying to piece things together. Step by step, Jess thought over everything that had happened since her first night in the house. She had her suspect for the string of seemingly suicidal deaths, and she had the method. She was pretty sure the motives were adding up too, and a quick confirmation from the police database would probably finalise any nagging doubts.

But there was one thing left. That was her mysterious houseguest, with their changeable moods and their convenient arrival in her life, the night before she began her first shift in the Huntshire Police Force.

Treading lightly across her landing, Jess stole silently into her bedroom and stood looking down at her empty bed. For a moment, she just couldn't shake the picture of another figure standing here, watching her body while she slept.

She glanced at the bedside table, and something made her astral stomach plummet. Lying in the dust that lightly coated the wooden surface, was a clearly defined line - as though someone, absent-mindedly, had run a finger through it. Without thinking, Jess traced the line gently with her own fingertip.

In her mind, the figure formed more completely, standing slightly taller than she was. There was a dark, familiar scowl on its brow, which dissolved away into a haunted, pleading look.

'Danny?' Jess whispered, into the empty house.
Nothing replied.

19

Three days later, Jess looked up from her desk as Danny sloped in through the office door, heading for the kitchenette. Grant bustled past him, looking stressed. She had developed deeper circles around her eyes since taking over as acting sergeant, standing in for Davies as he continued to heal slowly from his ordeal in the barn.

'You picked a hell of a day to be late,' Grant snapped, and Danny grunted at her. 'Einstein's late too, it's not like him,' she fussed, and hurried out into the corridor.

Moments later, Jess looked up again as Danny placed a cup of tea in front of her. She felt her whole body tense as he sat down opposite her, but wanting to keep things under a sheen of normality, she gingerly picked up the peace offering and sipped it carefully.

It was a pretty good brew, and despite everything, Jess appreciated the pick-me-up to fuel her through the mountain of paperwork she was facing.

Then he carefully slid a plate across the desk to her, which Jess noticed had two slightly charred slices of toast on it. She felt her stomach contract instinctively, and not just from the acrid smell of the burnt bread.

She looked up at him and met his gaze, as he watched her levelly.

'Did you have nice rest days, Danny?' Jess asked pointedly, and he nodded.

'Yeah. Did you?' Danny responded casually, and she nodded cautiously back before returning to her paperwork. 'Did Einstein call?' he asked her suddenly, and Jess froze.

'He did not,' she said eventually, deliberately bending her head down over her paperwork and ignoring her tutor's continuous stare.

'Einstein's not picking up his phone,' Grant announced, striding back into the office. She looked annoyed, but there was a hint of anxiety in her voice. 'He's never late… we'll give it a bit longer before it's an actual concern for welfare though, no need to worry,' she continued, more to herself than the room at large.

Jess felt a shiver pass through her, and she looked up at Danny, who was now conspicuously bent over his own paperwork.

'Maybe we could swing by his place later, if there's any free time?' Jess offered to Grant, as the older officer bustled past. 'I'm sure he'll turn up though,' she added encouragingly, watching her tutor's face carefully as she did so. Danny's expression remained impassive, and after a long moment, Jess returned reluctantly to her workload.

The office around her remained busy but quiet. After a few minutes, Jess took a quick glance around at her colleagues, who were all thoroughly engaged with their work.

Quietly adjusting her screen position so that it couldn't be seen by prying eyes, Jess began to search the police database for the queries that still tumbled through her mind.

'*Bill James, Dovecote Road,*' she typed first, scrolling through entries to pull out things she was looking for. The sexual assault case, a not-guilty verdict, and a closed investigation... closed by its investigating officer, PC Danny Jackson.

'*Terry Haines, Waites Gym,*' she tried next, and balked a little at the investigation she found into suspected downloading of child pornography. Once again, a not-guilty, once again the case was closed. Once again, PC Danny Jackson's name was there, this time countersigning the witness statement.

'*Shane Wilson, Priory House,*' she continued, fingers flying over the keys, eyes racing over the screen. It was no surprise that Danny Jackson seemed to have attended plenty of the call-outs to Shane and Ginny's flat.

'*Faye Parker,*' she tried, and somehow it was far worse when all she found was a witness statement and the death paperwork. Her own name on the witness statement this time, next to poor Faye's. Her vision blurred a little her eyes scanned the documents, putting together the brief story of a young woman who had done nothing worse than watching the wrong CCTV at the wrong time, and attracted the attention of a killer with tracks to cover.

She finally closed the database, trying desperately to look unruffled under the sharp glare of the fluorescent lights overhead.

'Danny,' she said slowly, and her tutor looked up at her through the gap between their computer screens. 'What do you think is going to happen to Charlie Benson?'

'I don't know,' Danny shrugged, 'he normally manages to weasel out of absolutely everything, so I guess we'll find him back on the streets before long.'

'You don't think this time might have shaken him up a bit?' Jess asked, a sharp tone creeping into her voice. 'He might show some remorse, like Shane Wilson did?'

'If we're lucky,' Danny said placidly, looking back down at his paperwork, before nodding to Jess's own. 'Come on, Jess, if you work through all of that we can go and check on Einstein. Isn't that what you wanted?'

Jess nodded, eyes narrowing as Danny bent his head down again. But she carefully closed all of her searches and carried on with her work. She had almost hoped that something in there would tell her she was wrong, point out some hole in her logic. But it only confirmed the iron certainty in her gut.

Somehow it made it worse now that she could see the twisted path, leading to the lonely bodies who had finally met some kind of sick, final justice.

As Jess watched the man opposite her, calmly making his way through his tasks, she couldn't shake Faye from her mind. It seemed that simply standing in Danny's way was now enough to earn the ultimate punishment, and Jess had a horrible feeling that her tutor might be about to teach her something.

*

Hours later, the police car finally pulled up outside a small row of terraced houses. Jess and Danny stepped out of the car into the chilly evening air, and Jess looked up at the dark house in front of them, shivering.

Wordlessly, she headed up to the front door and knocked firmly.

'Einstein?' she called shakily, and then after a moment's silence, 'Max?'

She peered through the living room window, trying to see through the net curtains. The interior was gloomy, but she could have sworn things didn't quite look right inside.

The dark shapes of Einstein's possessions looked messy, which was perhaps to be expected from an officer who couldn't keep his uniform tidy, but the strewn objects looked more like they had been tipped - or thrown.

Jess turned back to see Danny leaning against the car, watching her. She walked slowly back towards him, feeling her hands curl slowly into fists.

'Do you think we should call him again?' she asked, and Danny shrugged.

Jess turned back to look at the house, with its coldly unlit windows. She bit her lip and looked up at her tutor's calm expression.

'I… would like to look inside, if you have any supplies,' Jess said carefully. Danny looked down at her, his expression still unreadable.

'Sure,' he offered. His easy response only made her tension grow, as she looked up at the silently brooding house.

A few minutes later, Jess's projection slowly stepped through the solid bulk of Einstein's front door, arriving soundlessly in the hallway. She moved quickly through the dark rooms downstairs, peering into corners, and finding nothing but tumbled piles of magazines, old cans, dirty plates and the occasional odd sock. The furniture was definitely in disarray, and two bookshelves had actually been toppled onto their sides on the dark carpet.

She headed for the staircase and began to clamber upwards, keeping one eye on the dim hallway behind her as she climbed. Reaching the top, she stared straight down the corridor towards an ominously open door at the other end.

She moved carefully down the hall, glancing left and right at the closed doors to either side of her and heading straight for what she guessed was the bathroom, based on the narrow sliver of tiled wall she could see beyond. As she approached, she noticed that the white tile was splashed with something, which in the blue-tinged world of her projection looked for a moment like some kind of heavy, dark paint.

When she stepped through the bathroom door, Jess realised exactly what it was.

The first thing she noticed were the flies, buzzing lazily around the room, having come in from the window which must have been cracked open to let out steam from the bath. But any steam from the cold, still water in the tub had long since evaporated, and the wrinkled, pallid occupant inside was unlikely to care.

Einstein lay, glassy eyed, floating slightly in the cool water. The long, jagged gashes in his wrists had sprayed the room so completely with his dying blood that his pale body stuck out ghostly white against the wide, dark smears around him. Razor blades lay rusting on the tub's edge, caked in yet more of it.

Jess felt her throat constrict, desperately unsure whether to gag or cry. She moved instinctively towards Einstein's lonely corpse, reaching out towards him.

'Jess?' a voice asked, and she turned on her heel to see Danny, standing in the doorway to the bathroom. He was staring straight at her, and it took her a moment to realise he must have projected, before following her inside. She looked numbly back at him, her lip trembling.

'Jess, it's OK, it's OK,' Danny murmured, and walked towards her, his arms outstretched. He gathered her into them, and she froze against him in shock, not really knowing what to do.

Jess turned her face away from Danny as he clasped her close. Looking back towards the stained bathtub, she could see Einstein still floating there in the water, cold and alone.

'I've got you,' Danny crooned gently into her ear, as the flies buzzed around them, and the cold realisation sank even deeper into Jess's bones. 'I've got you.'

20

T he following days passed in both a blur and a crawl. Jess and Danny had been signed off work after the discovery of Einstein's gruesome corpse, and so she found herself facing her colleagues for the first time in a week as she walked quietly into the crematorium chapel.

As her small black heels clicked on the floor, she noticed faces turning to look at her, recognising other officers from the station. There were gentle whispers as she passed, generally sympathetic, all curious. Jess ignored them and headed for the large form of Sergeant Davies. He stooped slightly as he stood on crutches, but still loomed high over the rest of B Shift as they huddled together in a row.

They had all acquired smart black suits for the occasion, even Hunter and Packer, the latter of whom looked unusually grave as she grimaced sadly at Jess.

The Sergeant looked down at her as she edged

into the row beside him.

'You OK, Layton?' he asked her softly, and she nodded stiffly, trying to keep her eyes dry. He nodded back, still standing smartly despite his heavily bandaged leg.

Then another black-suited figure was suddenly moving in beside them, squeezing past the Sergeant, coming to stand directly next to Jess.

The faint smell of Danny's aftershave made Jess feel slightly sick as he stood beside her. Around her, B Shift were murmuring quiet greetings, but she couldn't bring herself to meet his eye. She looked down at their shoes instead. She'd never seen Danny wear such a smart pair of shoes. Somehow, that bothered her even more.

Then the music started, and the funeral began.

Jess kept her eyes fixed firmly on the beautiful stained glass at the front of the crematorium as the coffin moved past her, trying furiously not to cry. As the crowd rose and sat between hymns and moving words of remembrance from Einstein's devastated friends and family, Jess concentrated on keeping her breathing steady.

As the service finally drew towards its close, and they stood one last time for the coffin to retreat behind the curtains, Jess clenched her fists and dropped her head, unable to watch.

She felt the gentle touch of fingers brushing against her own, trying to tease her hand open, and she looked down to see Danny reaching for her, clearly hoping to hold her hand. She snatched it away, folding her arms tight across her chest and staring back at the stained glass again, as Danny glowered beside her.

Jess concentrated as hard as she could on the sunlight pouring in coloured streams through the window. She tried desperately not to hear the sound of Einstein's mother sobbing as the coffin vanished from view, before finally letting her own tears gush towards the crematorium floor.

*

Outside the crematorium, in the quiet hush of the gardens, B Shift stood huddled together. As Jess approached, her colleagues looked up and the little group parted, watching her sympathetically.

'We miss you at work, Jess,' Grant told her warmly, and the others nodded.

'Not just because we've got a shit-ton more paperwork to do without you, either,' Packer joked weakly, and Jess smiled faintly back.

'Just keep resting up,' Sergeant Davies rumbled, 'we only want you to come back when you're ready.'

Jess glanced over to where Danny stood alone, staring out into the crematorium gardens. He didn't seem as intimidating somehow, out here in the bright sunshine. She dragged her gaze away, back to the worried expressions of her colleagues.

'Thanks, guys. I'm sure I'll be ready soon,' she told them, and with one last nod, turned and walked towards the lone figure of her tutor, whose shadow stretched long over the whispering grass.

She arrived next to him and stood gazing out into the garden, squinting slightly in the late afternoon sun.

'Want to go home?' she asked him. Danny turned to her, a faint look of pleasant surprise passing across his face. He nodded, and they turned together, walking away across the car park.

Jess carefully kept a couple of paces behind him, watching his back as he strode away between the clustered mourners. Danny didn't even look up as they passed Einstein's mother, who sat shakily on a bench, being comforted by a small knot of family members.

Jess felt her resolve stiffen as she walked, but the sound of quiet crying continued to haunt her as they strode away. The tarmac of the carpark glowed softly in the sun, as an evening breeze began to ruffle the trees around them, and Jess and Danny's shadows grew steadily longer behind them.

*

As Jess sat on Danny's sofa, staring blankly at the wall ahead, she was jolted out of her reverie by the sound of her phone chiming from her bag.

She shook herself slightly and reached for it, pulling it out and feeling her stomach twist as she looked down at the image onscreen. She quickly reached up to try and rub any trace of smudged mascara away from her eyes, before plastering on a bright smile and picking up the video call.

'Mum!' Jess muttered, trying to keep her voice bright, while also remaining quiet enough that she wouldn't be heard in the next room. 'This really isn't a great time. Can I call you back?'

'Is everything OK, honey?' her mother asked immediately, frowning up at her with concern. 'Have you been crying?'

'Look – I've been at a funeral, Mum, it's kind of a long story,' Jess started, as her mother gasped in sympathy.

'Oh, Jess, I'm so sorry. Are you OK?'

'I'm fine, honestly, I'm fine. It's just not a great time. I know, I said I would call – things are really busy, but I'm OK. Work is – work is very busy, doing lots of overtime. But I'll call soon, we can catch up properly, OK? Maybe I'll come home for a bit?'

'OK, honey – or I can come to you, if you're really busy? You know I don't mind –' Alex began, but Jess shook her head. The last thing she wanted was to give Danny Jackson any more opportunities to interact with someone she cared about.

'I'm sorry, Mum, not right now. I've got to go,' Jess insisted, as Alex opened her mouth to speak again. 'Bye, Mum.'

'I love you, Jess. I'm here whenever you need me,' her mother told her quietly. Jess nodded, feeling her eyes grow hot and teary again.

'I know. I love you too,' she replied, and shut the

phone off, taking a deep, calming breath.

As she sat on the sofa, still clutching the phone in her hand, she heard soft footsteps approaching down the hallway, and the slow creak of the living room door being pushed open.

She finally looked up to see Danny standing framed in the doorway, his face in shadow as he stood just outside the warm light of the lounge. His eyes glittered as he peered down at her phone.

'Who was that?' he asked softly, and Jess shook her head slightly.

'Oh, it wasn't anything important,' she insisted firmly, 'I might head to bed early, I think.'

Jess stood up from the sofa and faced him, but Danny made no motion to leave the doorway.

'OK. Aren't you going to have dinner with me, first?' he asked, narrowing his eyes at her, and Jess nodded slowly.

'Yeah. OK. Dinner, then bed, I reckon. Sounds – sounds good,' she mumbled, feeling an aching tiredness flow through her bones as she stood awkwardly under his watchful gaze.

He finally stood to one side, and she dropped her head and walked quietly through the doorway, squeezing past him and heading for the kitchen. As she passed, she was fairly sure she saw the trace of a smile flicker across his face.

*

Jess was quietly relieved when Danny decided

on an early night, sloping away to his room almost as soon as dinner was over.

She still made a careful show of clattering around the kitchen for a while, loading the dishwasher, pouring herself a final glass of water, then padding noticeably about in the lounge as she prepared the sofa for another restless night.

As she finally settled down in the blanket, she was pretty sure the house was now otherwise completely still. She clicked off the lamp beside her, staring up at the dark ceiling, listening intently for the now-familiar creaks and groans of the bungalow. After a few minutes, she was satisfied that her moment had arrived.

On feather-light feet, she trod gently to the living room door, peering into the dark hallway. Danny's light was out. Jess hoped that if she was lucky, he had been lulled into the rhythm of their safe, dull routine, and was genuinely asleep.

Quickly, Jess crossed the room, trying desperately to make as little noise as possible. In a few practiced movements, she had raised one of the tall sash windows. She tucked the lace curtain back, exactly as she had on the night of her fateful visit to Shane and Ginny.

Without wasting a second more, she tiptoed back to the sofa and slid under the protective cover of her blanket, where she quietly withdrew one of her carefully hidden bottles. When she removed the stopper, the smell was almost intoxicating. She hadn't expected to miss it that much, but as she raised it to her lips, she realised she'd been craving the strange, heavy taste.

Her projection slipped silently out from her blanket, instantly searching every shadow for a sign of Danny. He didn't appear, and she felt her body relax for a moment.

For the first time in days, she felt genuinely alone.

This time she barely registered her subconscious change into police uniform, as she trod quickly back across the carpet to where the window waited for her. The dark garden outside faded into deep blackness on the astral plane, but the heady, sweet smell of the flowers was still so inviting. She ducked quickly down, and this time she was ready for the sharp shock as she brushed the sill.

But what she wasn't ready for, as her body cleared the narrow gap, was the net.

Jess yelled in surprise as she plunged unwittingly into its rippling silver surface. A crackling jolt of energy shot through her astral body, and she lost her footing as her back spasmed in shock.

As Danny stepped from the shadows, he yanked the mouth of the net closed, trapping Jess bodily in its folds. She howled as the burning pain coursed through her. Thoughts of Terry flashed through her mind, as she recalled the way he had moaned and writhed on the gym floor underneath the net, before Danny brought his short afterlife to an end.

Unfortunately for Jess, it seemed Danny wasn't quite done with her yet.

Her tutor deftly gathered the net up in his arms,

carrying Jess away from the window. He moved quickly, and Jess dimly realised that she must weigh almost nothing in this form, though Danny's arms were unnervingly solid as he gripped her through the net.

Before she knew it, he had carried her around to the back door, over the threshold and into the kitchen. As she tried to keep her mind straight in between the rippling waves of pain, Jess wondered wildly whether he had waited outside for her every night, or simply got lucky.

She hit the floor with a hard thump as Danny dropped the net onto the living room carpet, and she came to rest on her side, with a clear view of the sofa. Her body was still bundled up under the blanket, seemingly sleeping.

Danny reached out and gently pulled back the blanket, revealing her physical form. He stared down at it for a long moment, and then turned to the net, focusing on a spot just a few inches from Jess's eyes.

'Did you really think that I didn't know you left through the window, the last time you slipped out of here?' he asked, sounding genuinely annoyed. 'You don't give me enough credit sometimes, Jess.'

She knew there was no point responding as he glared down at her. Jess concentrated on keeping as still as she could, hoping to stop brushing against the silvery folds as much as possible, minimising the pain. Her body felt like it was on fire where the net's fibres lay against her astral form, and each twisted rope seemed to be branding itself against her skin, even through her uniform.

'I keep trying to give you more chances,' Danny continued, his voice growing higher and wilder as he began to pace up and down in front of the sofa. 'You just can't seem to do what I ask, even though it really makes no sense… I don't want to hurt you, do you understand that?'

Jess felt like the net was closing in tighter around her as she watched his feet frantically pacing. Then they stopped and he turned back to the sofa, staring down at her physical body where it lay silent and unprotected.

'You know, maybe I like you better like this,' Danny said quietly, his face twisting into a wry smile that made Jess's spectral stomach twist. 'Maybe we should keep it this way for a while?'

'No!' Jess shouted, bucking against the net as he reached down towards her body. The silver fibres of the net burned harder as she hit them, and Jess grimaced in pain, tears beginning to stream down her face. The material must have rustled gently as she thrust against it, and Danny turned, looking down at her, still smiling horribly.

'All right Jess, calm down, you'll hurt yourself,' he sneered, and crouched down over the net. He was now inches away from her, but Jess couldn't reach him through the rippling, crackling folds. He gripped the fibres with one hand.

'If I let you out, you'd better behave yourself,' Danny continued mockingly, pausing with his hand enmeshed in the net. 'Tell you what - why don't you tap once for "yes"?'

Jess's anger reached a bubbling peak, and as it boiled over, she thought she saw her fingers elongate again. There they were, the animal hands, the claws. When she opened her eyes, without her knowing, they glowed.

She bucked against the net, hissing, her back on fire as she shoved against her gently rustling prison. Danny's eyes narrowed as he watched the net twitch, and something in the back of Jess's spectral mind fought back against the wild, feral forefront.

Jess had to get out of the net first, if she was going to do anything about Danny.

She raised one clawed hand and thumped it hard into the floor, crushing the net against it, and howled as pain coursed through her arm. Danny was smiling slightly now, almost relaxing for a moment, the grip of his fingers slackening against the net.

Underneath it, Jess grinned, and her teeth were sharp.

Then, her energy spent, she dropped prone and moaned softly as her back continued to burn.

Slowly, Danny gripped the net again, and finally whipped it back. Cool air rushed to fill the burning void, and Jess breathed deeply, calming herself. The long fingers withdrew, her eyes were brown again. She crawled across the carpet on trembling hands and knees, getting herself clear of the net.

Jess looked up at Danny, and her glare was

diamond hard. Although the anger still bubbled away inside her, there was also a hint of smug satisfaction as she watched his chest anxiously rise and fall. It gave her the fire she needed to haul her throbbing astral body upright, and then stand up shakily.

For a moment, she looked over to where her unconscious physical form lay on the sofa. Then her gaze slid back to Danny, who was watching it carefully, clearly waiting for her to wake.

She had seen enough in Shane and Ginny's flat to know what happened here if she stayed. But as she glanced over her shoulder, to where the sash window still gaped open to the dark garden beyond, she knew she had one key advantage.

Danny still thought he was in control.

Jess ran on shaking legs to the window and hurled herself through. This time the crackle of the sage and silver felt like barely a breath compared to her already burning skin. She heaved herself out through the garden, her boots pounding the grass as she began to find her footing again.

Jess staggered out into the dark, silent street, watching the bungalow carefully over her shoulder. Light poured from the windows, and she carefully eyed every exit, waiting for her pursuer to emerge.

Unsurprisingly, when he did so, he didn't cast a shadow.

Danny ducked out through the same window, crossing the garden and standing carefully at the edge of the lawn. Jess turned to face him, drawing herself upright and feeling the burning sensation in her limbs slowly subside into a low, throbbing ache.

They regarded each other silently for a long moment, as they waited in between the deep blue pools of streetlight.

'So, I assume it's pointless to tell you that I know what you've been doing?' Jess began, and Danny's lip curled.

'I was going to tell you. Eventually. Once you'd got used to the idea,' he told her, and Jess's eyes narrowed.

'How thoughtful,' she replied dryly. 'So, you were hoping I'd end up as your assistant? Or should I say accomplice? Or was it something else you wanted?'

Danny's lip twitched for a moment, but he didn't reply. His eyes flickered over Jess's body for a moment, and she felt the anger rise again as his gaze raked her.

Her tutor seemed to be relaxing a little as they talked, but Jess noticed his fists were curled. Her own hands were tight with tension, and she felt every spectral muscle in her legs contract with nervous energy, ready to fire.

'You know what I wanted, Jess,' he said quietly, and for a moment the tension in her body was released in a sudden shiver.

'Did you really think all this was the way to get it?' she asked eventually, trying to keep her voice even. Danny took a step towards her, and she tensed again, but held her ground.

'Just think what I'm offering you, Jess,' he murmured. His eyes were wide and glinted ominously in the astral moonlight. 'I've shown you more than most people get to see in their lifetime. Do you have any idea how lucky you are?

'When they told me who my first tutee was, I couldn't believe it,' he continued, his voice growing louder with excitement. 'You were this young, single woman who'd moved halfway across the country, it seemed as though you were practically screaming to be recruited into projection. I just couldn't resist taking a look at you before our first shift together.'

'So that's why you broke into my house?' Jess asked coldly.

Danny laughed. It was a high, wavering laugh that set Jess's teeth on edge.

'Broke in? I walked in, Jess. That's what this is,' he cried, 'it's the ability - the *power* to do what you want to do. And we want the same thing,' he insisted. Jess's eyes narrowed.

'What's that?' she snapped, and Danny grinned wildly back at her.

'Justice, Jess. You wanted to be a police officer, you wanted to bring justice... but you've seen it yourself, half of the time even the police are powerless. But we don't have to be! We can do so much more –'

'Danny, I know you think all this was justified,' Jess interrupted firmly. 'I know you believe that chasing down criminals who "got away with it" was the right thing to do, making some sick example out of them… I think what I'm trying to say is that I follow the logic. But surely you can see that what you're doing is a crime.'

'Oh, come on,' Danny scoffed, rolling his eyes. 'Surely you can see that there's a difference between legality and morality?'

'Well that's an interesting point,' Jess snapped. 'Let's examine this from the top, shall we? Or at least, from the parts I know about. After you decided to stalk me, you then chased me out of my own home. Presumably so I would have to call a psychic?'

'Very astute, Jess,' Danny sneered.

'I mean, it's lucky I actually picked you, isn't it? What if I'd fucked off with some other ghost-botherer?'

'I mean, we're the only genuine mediums in about fifty miles, so I knew you'd come to me eventually,' Danny sniffed, and Jess rolled her eyes.

'Are you not even slightly sorry?' she asked quietly, and Danny paused, considering her for a long moment.

'Jess, I never wanted to hurt you. And it hurts me, that you can't see everything I'm trying to do for you. I only ever wanted to make sure you were safe, and get to know you better, so I could show you how much I cared about you. I wanted to understand your life, see what you liked to eat, what you liked to wear, what radio station you liked to listen to…' Danny rambled, and he stepped towards Jess again, his face twisting into a terrible, ingratiating smile.

'You must have been so pleased with yourself, when you heard me send that message to Bill James through the radio,' Jess snorted bitterly, and Danny's pleading smile faltered.

'Pleased? Jess, I was so disappointed,' he told her, shaking his head sadly. 'I should have been the one to tell you. But I understand. You were angry, I hadn't let you in, I should have told you sooner so that you could see what I was trying to do,' Danny continued, and he moved forwards again. It took all Jess's courage not to bolt, as his eyes blazed into her from just a few feet away.

'Danny, you withholding the truth from me is currently at the bottom of a list of offences, which include invading bodies, murdering acquitted criminals and at least one completely innocent witness, and… and killing a fellow police officer,' Jess said angrily, her voice cracking a little on the final words.

Danny didn't say anything, but just continued to watch her with an unwavering stare.

'Was it just because you thought he would take me away from you?' Jess asked eventually, feeling tears prick the corners of her astral eyes. 'In case you hadn't noticed, Danny, I'm the one who chose to leave. You didn't have to hurt him!'

'Maybe if you'd listened to me, I wouldn't have had to hurt him,' Danny countered, and Jess shook her head.

'You know what? I'm sorry I didn't try to keep

him away from me, so he'd be safe. But I'm still not the one who killed him, Danny,' Jess cried, stepping forwards into the dark road, closing the gap between them. 'What did you think was going to happen here? Did you think that you needed to break me, so I'd do what you say? What exactly was it that you wanted me to do?'

'I needed someone to catch the spirits after I'd finished with their bodies,' Danny told her bluntly, and Jess stopped in her tracks, gaping at him. 'I kept losing them, and it was a mess going back to clean up. I mean, that's what I planned at first. But then you arrived, and I don't know… I suddenly realised I could have so much more than that. I could have a proper partner, someone who shared my passion,' Danny insisted, and with one final step forwards, he was now just inches from Jess's face.

'Well, despite your sinister method of research, you found the wrong person,' Jess told him quietly, her gaze steady as she met his crazed, pleading stare.

'So it seems,' Danny replied bluntly. For a moment, he looked genuinely upset. Then he turned on his heel and moved back towards the bungalow.

Jess stood in the dark road, realising that her spectral heart was pounding hard in her chest, and she tried to calm her jagged breathing.

Then a cold understanding flooded through her, and Jess started to run back towards the building. As she thundered down the path, the front door swung back open and Danny emerged, back in his physical form. Skidding to a halt in front of him, Jess looked down at what he held in his arms. Tightly wrapped in the silver net was Jess's own physical body, still fast asleep.

Danny walked purposefully towards her, and Jess shrank back into the dark shadows of the garden. She had seen this determined stride before, on a grainy CCTV image, as Terry's possessed body headed straight for its final, choking breaths.

As she watched Danny curl his arms tighter around her slumbering body, her mind was full of churning images. Bill hanging from a warehouse balcony, his neck bruised and eerily elongated. Terry covered in crusting vomit, slumped against the sinks. Finally Einstein, floating cold and alone, surrounded by frantic sprays of his own blood.

Jess felt sure she was about to discover what Danny intended for her own final punishment.

Whatever he had planned, it seemed Danny wasn't stupid enough to do it in the house. As he walked out into the street, she noticed that he headed for Jess's car, unlocking it with the keys he must have stolen from her bag.

Danny stowed her body quickly inside, and as he turned away, she realised he now wore the tactical gloves, preventing him from leaving fingerprints. She almost had to hand it to him, Danny Jackson was at least pretty good at what he did.

All Jess could hope for, as she slid silently through the side of the car and into the seat behind him, was that she was better.

21

J ess didn't know what to expect as she rode silently in the back seat of her own car, being taken street by street, further away from the bungalow.

Streetlights and headlights streamed endlessly through the car windows, illuminating the seat where Jess cast no shadow against the worn fabric. She found herself gazing numbly out into the night, remembering the long, moonlit car ride when she had driven with her mother to visit her new hometown for the first time.

Her stomach twisted as she thought about her phone, still sitting in the lounge of the bungalow. She wished more than anything that she had thought to send one final message. Jess couldn't bear the idea that after tonight was over, her mother would be told that she had taken her own life.

Familiar roads connected together until the vehicle finally drew to a halt on the edge of a still, silent farm. As the dark buildings came into view, Jess realised that she recognised this place.

Her lip curled slightly as she left the car and looked up at the dark barn ahead, brooding at the other end of the field. Danny had at least picked a poetic location for her final moments.

He hauled her body from the car, carrying it gently in his arms, the net rustling quietly around her. The large, familiar bulk of the black kit bag bounced gently against Danny's back as he walked.

Jess trod silently behind him across the whispering blades of grass, as Danny strode confidently ahead, towards the looming bulk of the barn. Now the field was cleared of the screaming horde of police vehicles and bustling bodies, it seemed empty and cold, particularly in the glowing blue light of the astral plane.

As they reached the barn, one massive door stood slightly ajar, behind the lines of leftover police tape that rippled eerily in the breeze. Jess watched Danny slip past them, heading for the gap, and she wondered how long he might have been planning this.

He disappeared into the darkness beyond the doors, and Jess's feet dragged instinctively to a halt as she stood outside, savouring one final moment where she could smell the damp grass around her boots and feel the chill of the night air. The sensations seemed sadly muted to her spectral body.

As she hesitated, Jess found herself questioning if there were other times that he had considered bringing her here. For a moment, she had the unbearable thought that had she pushed him just a little harder, he might have taken her here weeks ago instead of visiting Einstein.

Taking one last look down at her astral self, there was something comforting about the police uniform she wore. Jess knew that she might not live long enough to be officially signed off as an officer, but there was no question that the job was a part of her now.

Jess looked back up into the darkness, then stepped smokily through the door. She gasped as she took in the scene inside.

The chaos of the fight was still in evidence, whether due to ongoing investigation or simply neglect on the part of the owner. But there was one feature Jess definitely didn't remember.

As she stood by the door, staring dead ahead, she could see a lamp had been placed on the floor, illuminating the forest of boxes and machinery around it. Directly above the lamp, hanging ominously from the metal balcony, was a stiff, hemp rope. Its end was twisted into a noose.

'I hope you made it, Jess,' Danny called, walking quietly across the dark, dusty floor. 'Not everyone gets to watch themselves die.'

'When did you do this?' Jess whispered into the oppressive hush of the barn.

Danny, unhearing, continued to walk.

As he drew level with the noose, Danny laid her body down gently on the ground, and it rolled limply inside the silvery folds of the net. Jess trod slowly forwards, watching, waiting for her opportunity. She hesitated as her tutor reached carefully into the kit bag, withdrawing a bottle and giving a last glance around him, as though trying to discern where Jess might be.

Trying not to disturb any dust, Jess crept around him, circling, coming to a stop directly in front of his unseeing eyes. She glanced down at the kit bag which nestled by her feet, and her spectral pulse thudded as she noticed the hilt of the dagger, gleaming in the gap between the tough black fabric.

Jess looked across to where her body lay slumped beneath the net. If she was correct in her assumption of what was about to happen, she might have only seconds in which to act, and Danny was clearly well-practiced in his method. Still, he'd never gone up against a spirit that knew what it was in for.

As Danny uncorked his bottle and laid a hand on the net, Jess crouched opposite him, ready to spring.

Danny whipped the net back, drank, swallowed, and collapsed forwards in a crumpled heap next to Jess's exposed body. As she stared, her tutor's projection unfolded slowly.

For a moment, Jess was distracted, as she realised that she had never truly watched a spirit leave its body. A shimmering mass was rippling out from Danny's slumped form, gradually taking on human features until it formed into a perfect copy of the man in front of her. There was no police uniform on Danny Jackson, but Jess was hardly surprised.

The projection opened its eyes, and Jess lunged.

She hit Danny's spirit fully in the chest, sending him tumbling backwards, away from where their physical bodies lay sprawled on the dirty floor. Dust swirled around them as the two projections thumped against the ground, grappling wildly with one another.

Danny rolled Jess onto her back, one hand clawing for her neck. Jess thrust her hand upwards into his face, shoving his head backwards until he lost his grip. She twisted sideways beneath him, so when his hand plunged down to catch her throat, it hit the floor instead.

As Danny's concentration slipped, Jess reached her arm around him and shoved hard, dislodging his position and allowing her to wriggle free. He fell forwards onto the ground, and Jess threw herself sideways, landing on top of Danny's back and pinning him to the floor.

Her tutor's strength caught her by surprise as he planted his hands on the ground and reared up onto his knees. Jess scrabbled furiously behind him, trying to pin his arms, but Danny was too quick for her. His right elbow flew up and caught Jess sharply in the stomach.

She gasped and released him for a moment, just long enough for him to go scrambling furiously back towards the bodies on his hands and knees. Then Jess grabbed Danny's ankle and yanked him hard, dragging a long line through the dust.

He took a moment to catch his breath and Jess

hurtled forwards, overtaking him, diving headlong for her own body and plunging deep inside it as she landed roughly on the floor. She pulled her limbs frantically into what she hoped were the right positions, feeling her consciousness sinking, closing her spectral eyes. She heard Danny scrabble forwards behind her, then silence.

When she opened her eyes again, she was back in her physical form. She could feel the soft cotton of her pyjamas against her skin, and the sharp sensation of the gravel and debris on the barn floor pressing through the fabric.

Danny still lay prone beside her. Jess reached immediately for the net, flinging it over Danny's physical body and grinning as it settled around him. Then she hauled herself to her feet, nerves firing wildly, eyes flicking around the dark, still barn.

For a moment, nothing moved except the swirling, churning dust.

Then something reached up and grabbed her, hard, around the neck. Jess reached up, grappling wildly with unseen hands as they clutched harder. She felt her windpipe stutter closed as the fingers gripped her throat. Jess couldn't breathe, and as she began to panic, her mouth opened, desperately trying to suck in oxygen.

She suddenly recognised the heady, earthy, salty smell as a small bottle was thrust roughly into her open mouth. Jess gagged as the contents hit the back of her throat. The unseen hands rammed her jaw closed, and she instinctively swallowed, cursing silently as her body dropped back to the dusty floor.

When Jess woke, panting, a few feet away from herself, there was no sign of Danny. For a moment she simply watched as her own body sprawled on the floor of the barn, its shadow pooling long and dark in the harsh beam of light thrown by the lantern.

Then slowly, shakily, her body stood up. It was facing away from her, gazing up at the rope as it hung ominously in the dusty air. As it took a hesitant step forwards, Jess found herself moving too, walking carefully around until she finally came to a halt in front of her own, living face.

Except it wasn't hers, now. She felt the same shiver run through her as the moment she had seen Terry re-emerge on the CCTV. Just as his body had looked suddenly different in the way it strode across the lonely gym, this young woman simply wasn't Jess anymore. The way the mouth curled cruelly at the corner, the way the shoulders hunched a little more than usual, the way the brow seemed heavier and darker.

Jess stood frozen in the darkness, her mind racing as she watched her own body grab a metal chair, drag it across the floor, and position it carefully under the noose.

She began to step forwards, but then stopped again, fists curling in frustration. All she could think to do was grab a bottle from the bag, thrust it into her own physical mouth, kick Danny out - and then what? Go through the whole thing again, until they ran out of projection fluid, or did something more drastic?

'You can still stop this, Jess. I just need to know you're going to behave,' her body called into the darkness, as the chair's legs clanged into place on the floor. Jess watched herself clamber up to stand on top of the chair.

'You know, this barn is one of the few places I didn't follow you,' Danny continued, his words sounding stilted as they came from Jess's physical mouth. Even her accent had changed, tinged with Danny's touch of Estuary English. 'But I saw the men who walked out of here. That's the day I knew I couldn't let you go. There's something in you, Jess, something we share. More than just this body,' Danny told her, and he raised Jess's physical hands, touching her face, her neck, her hair.

In the darkness, Jess's scowl was thunderous as she watched her own hands rake across her skin, moving down to touch her breasts through the thin fabric of her pyjamas. Jess's spectral eyes blazed with anger, as she watched her physical ones flutter slightly in enjoyment. Danny was loving this.

'So, what's it going to be, Jess?' Danny asked. The tone was quiet, but every syllable cut through the whirling dust and echoed slightly in the huge, cold space. 'You can either learn to live with me... or don't.'

Then Jess watched as her body gripped the thick, heavy rope, and draped it around her neck.

Silence rang around the barn for a long moment,

as Jess stood, regarding her physical self. The rope hung slack, but there was something unnerving about the way it twitched a little with every breath her body took.

'Tell you what, why don't you tap once for "sorry",' Danny continued mockingly, and twisted Jess's mouth into a sick smile.

Jess bristled, and then slowly picked up a thick piece of metal pole that lay discarded on the floor. It was heavy for her astral form to shift, but she gripped it determinedly in her spectral fists, and raised it up to shoulder height. Then she brought it around in a soaring arc, thumping it hard into a tall metal support that soared up into the darkness above them.

The clanging sound rocketed around the barn, and her body whipped around, staring at the pole as it hovered, still ringing in Jess's astral hands. Then Jess dropped the pole on the ground with a dusty thud.

'Very good, Jess,' Danny sneered. 'Maybe I should let you come home again, after all. But while I've got you, I just want to make sure you don't forget how to behave in future.'

Danny raised Jess's left hand. Then he raised her right hand and gripped her left ring finger.

He twisted it back, hard.

The sound of her own body screaming made Jess's spectral form panic, and she ran wildly forwards through the dust, eyes wide and staring as she watched her body raise its hands again. Danny gripped her middle finger. He twisted, and this time Jess was close enough to hear the tearing snap.

Another scream echoed around the space.

'Stop!' Jess cried, and as she skidded to a halt beside the chair, she grabbed at her own physical arms, wrestling them down. She looked down at her body's left hand, whose wrist she was holding tight in her spectral grip. It looked bizarre, with two fingers bent at strange angles, the flesh around them already starting to swell.

She looked up at her own face, which was staring straight over her astral shoulder. It was grinning, a horrible grin that Jess could never have imagined seeing on her own face.

Jess let go of her arms, and Danny let them drop back to her physical sides. He was clearly in agony, as tears poured down Jess's face, and the grin twitched unnervingly into a grimace.

For a long moment, Jess stood and watched herself in the deep, blue shadows of the barn. Her body looked thin and tired in the shabby pyjamas, and her expression was rapidly twisting into a tight knot of pain. The fingers on her left hand were still swelling as they hung crookedly by her side.

'Are we done here, Jess?' Danny asked suddenly, and Jess heard a tremor in the voice this time. It sounded smaller, and younger, and a little frightened.

Danny reached up with her good right hand, and slowly grasped the hemp rope around her neck, fingers twitching nervously. It looked like he might be changing his mind.

But Jess had made her decision.

She cast no shadow as she stood in the harsh blue glow, looking up at her own face as it began to twist in fear and pain. Her physical hand gripped the rope.

Then her spectral boot kicked the chair away.

As her body lost its footing, her legs swung wildly in the air. The thick rope yanked taught. There was a terrible, gasping, choking sound as Jess's body unsuccessfully tried to suck in oxygen, her hands clawing frantically at her pockets, the good right hand pulling free a tiny bottle, the broken fingers of the left desperately grappling with the cork.

The cork finally came free, and Danny tried to force the liquid into Jess's dying mouth. But her physical hands were trembling too much with the jerking, twitching motion of her body, and the bottle slipped, tumbling to the ground.

A sudden shadow appeared on the floor of the barn, as the ornate dagger rose into the air, drifting ethereally through the dust that whirled around Jess's frantically kicking legs. The scabbard slipped free, and the blade glinted ominously in the lamp-light.

On the astral plane, Jess gripped the hilt, looking up at her own, dying face. She knew she had little time left to decide, but she didn't need it.

Striding forwards, Jess thrust the dagger home. As it sank deep into her stomach, the body hanging above her went limp, the eyes glassy, and she felt a strange rush in the swirling dust, followed by a strong smell of sage and silver.

Danny was gone.

The body swung in the air, now hanging limply from the rope above, and Jess Layton stood in silence for a moment, watching her corpse come slowly to rest. Then she shook herself from her reverie and stepped into the darkness, where Danny's slumbering body lay. It would never be used by its former occupant again.

She leaned down and thrust her hands into the burning folds of the silver net. Inch by agonising inch, she dragged it sideways, before letting it pool onto the dirty floor.

Danny's body now lay exposed before her, as Jess breathed heavily, trying to ignore the throbbing pain coursing up her forearms. She reached for the dagger again, bent down across his peaceful form, and drew deep lines into his unconscious wrists.

Thick blood gushed frantically onto the floor of the barn as Danny's body slumbered on, breathing growing steadily shallower as Jess worked. She tucked the hilt of the dagger carefully into his gloved hand, wrapping his fingers firmly around it, while avoiding the wickedly sharp tip.

Then she dragged her hands across the dusty floor, creating swirling shapes in the dirt, before heading back to the kit bag and drawing out Danny's phone.

She lifted his dying finger, still slightly warm,

and dialled '999' on the touchscreen. The sound of the call connecting over speakerphone shattered the silence in the dark barn.

As she walked away, her boots made no impression on the letters she had written in the dust. Behind her stretched the words:

DON'T TOUCH THE BLADE

Jess didn't need any more deaths on her spectral hands tonight.

In the empty barn, the phone continued to ring, then was picked up at the other end with a crackle.

'Operator, what's your emergency?' called a faint voice. After a moment, it repeated, 'Hello? What's your emergency?'

A stack of boxes crashed suddenly onto the ground, as though struck by some invisible hand, and the unseen operator swiftly began dispatching emergency vehicles.

Dust continued to swirl in the dark interior of the barn, as Nothing left silently through the doorway, and out into the night.

EPILOGUE

Three months later, Charlie Benson emerged from court into the dying evening sunlight, flanked by his lawyers, and a collection of mysterious, hulking men who didn't look entirely at home in their smart suits.

His favourite camel-coloured coat billowed out from his shoulders as he strode down the street, heading for a row of large, immaculate cars, parked at one end of a dark alleyway.

'Ah, actually gents, I could really do with a slash. That judge didn't half go on a bit,' he announced, and his entourage obediently began piling into the cars while Charlie wandered off into the alleyway.

Reaching a spot of mild privacy behind a row of bins, he unzipped his expensive trousers, and began the luxuriant piss of a free man. As he finished, he breathed a deep sigh of satisfaction and zipped himself back up.

In fact, Charlie had been so absorbed in his own

urination, he had totally failed to notice a bin rising slowly into the air behind him.

With a thoroughly satisfying crash, the bin caught him squarely to the side of the head, sending Charlie and his best courtroom suit sprawling directly into the puddle of fresh urine on the muddy ground.

He struggled furiously in the dirt but failed to see his assailant as she walked away, spectral boots making no sound as they strode confidently away into the night.

Jess Layton grinned as she moved into the deep shadows of the astral plane. The mostly black uniform of the Huntshire Police Force blended almost perfectly into her surroundings, but no eyes could see her tonight as she disappeared silently from the alleyway.

She didn't know exactly what justice looked like on this side of the afterlife, but she was definitely going to enjoy finding it.

Jess Layton will return,
in Part Two of the Graveyard Shift Trilogy

Thank you for choosing to support this independent book project. Books like this survive thanks to readers like you, and they grow from their readers too.

So, if you want to read more by Bex Kilburn, please consider leaving a review and telling your friends, family, and anyone who will listen to buy a copy.

I really hope you've enjoyed it.

@bexkilburn

www.bexkilburn.co.uk

ACKNOWLEDGMENTS

W hile writing this book, I made the lovely discovery that becoming an author doesn't actually have to mean working alone.

Along the way, so many people have given their time, effort and support to what would otherwise have been a lonely and difficult process. So, I have the nice problem of needing to fit quite a lot of thanks into these final pages.

Firstly, thanks are due to the original cast and crew of the short film that started *Off Duty*. They came for back-to-back night shoots in a chilly warehouse in Basildon, and poured so much energy and enthusiasm into making our little story not only come to life, but tour around the world on cinema screens big and small.

So, to Jamie, Chloe, Rozi, Sam, Callum, Sam, Tom and Oliver, thank you so much for starting this journey.

Particular thanks also go to Tom, for not only being part of that team and playing my original on-screen Bill James, but also all your unwavering support and hard work to help my stories come to life.

To all the festivals who screened *Off Duty*, and played a huge role in keeping me going through the early days of learning how to tell a good story, thank you for all the effort you put into encouraging storytellers of all experience levels to keep honing their craft.

To Andy, thank you for keeping me company through the long evenings of writing, editing, sketching and generally putting this mammoth project together.

To Ellie, thank you for your invaluable feedback on the cover design. Your thoughts helped to turn it from something I liked into something I loved.

To Rosemary, Debbie and Tom, thank you for being among my first readers. Your views, edits and ideas shaped this book into a much better version of itself, and your words of encouragement kept me going through the final stages.

To all the friends and family who listened to my mad ramblings about wanting to write this book in the first place, thank you all so much for your patience and support.

Particular thanks go to Rosemary and Kevin for all of your advice, encouragement and help over the years, and to Katie, for listening to all my crazy ideas and always being my cheerleader. I hope I've done you proud.

Finally, the biggest thanks of all goes to Sam, for everything.

Printed in Great Britain
by Amazon